TRANSACTIONS OF BELONGING

Jaya Padmanabhan

PLATINUM PRESS

First published in India 2014 by Platinum Press
An imprint of Leadstart Publishing Pvt Ltd
1 Level, Trade Centre
Bandra Kurla Complex
Bandra (East) Mumbai 400 051 India
Telephone: +91-22-40700804
Fax: +91-22-40700800
Email: info@leadstartcorp.com
www.leadstartcorp.com

Sales Office:
Unit No.25/26, Building No.A/1,
Near Wadala RTO,
Wadala (East), Mumbai – 400037 India
Phone: +91 22 24046887

US Office:
Axis Corp, 7845 E Oakbrook Circle
Madison, WI 53717 USA

ISBN 978-93-83562-27-5

Cover Design Mishta Roy
Layout Chandravadan R. Shiroorkar
Typeset in Calibri
Printed at Printstop India Pvt Ltd, Mumbai

Price — India: Rs145; Elsewhere: US $6

Dedication

To my father, in honor of his passionate convictions.

To my mother, for your spunk and spirit.

About the Author

Jaya Padmanabhan has worked as a Copywriter, Sales Manager, Collections Agent, Software Engineer and Television Producer before emerging as a writer. She believes that her previous jobs distinctly inhabit her work. She has won three Katha Short Story Contest titles, the Lorian Hemingway Short Story recognition and the New America Media award for feature reporting. She lives in California with her husband, mother, twin girls and a Goldendoodle. She is the editor of India Currents magazine.

Acknowledgements

I'd like to thank Vidhya Subramanian who was the first to read the stories and validate them with the words: heck they are good; Vandana Kumar for applying her red pen and fierce honesty; my agent, Marc Parent, who took a chance on me; my daughter Kavya Padmanabhan who helped me frame some of the teenage voices in this collection; my daughter Prianca Padmanabhan for her quiet caring; my beloved husband, Ramesh Padmanabhan, for his steadfast support.

Contents

The Fly Swatter

Once, he had been asked at a job interview, "What do you expect to do with a history degree?" Rafat had answered, "become a teacher?" but the answer itself had become a question and it was only when he met Manu, the charismatic Minister of Social Justice, that he realized he wanted to *make history* instead.

The position of Fly Swatter had been created as a private joke, a snide reference to the impracticality of a history degree. It certainly wasn't like becoming an accountant like Gopi, his classmate from school, who was required to calibrate numbers all day long. Manu insisted that Rafat's business cards bore the title Fly Swatter to Manu Prasad, Minister of Social Justice. Thus was history made, for the position entered the annals of the 15th Bihar Legislative Assembly ledger when Cabinet Member Nitin Kumar had irately announced that the minister was getting above himself by hiring a fly swatter on government pay. This had pleased Manu no end and he had ordered a reprint of Rafat's business cards, adding a raised gold emboss to the title.

Rafat's paychecks bore the stamp of The Ministry of Social Justice. Each paycheck carried his name, salary and title. Rafat filed each stub in his desk drawer at home. In these uncertain times, history graduates from The National College of Patna were not particularly coveted. Each paystub validated and endorsed his job—a job like none other.

He spent the first few months learning the ropes, weaving his way through the jungle of influence that surrounded Manu, armed with his fly swatter's fan that he'd been instructed to carry at all times. But it was only since the night he'd sat behind Minister Manu in his black Mercedes and encountered a volatile group of young men seeking communal revenge with bricks and sticks that Rafat recognized the true elaboration of Manu's magnetism. The radio reports briefly touched upon some riots near the Buxar region and Manu instructed the chauffeur Harlal to drive towards Buxar. Upon reaching the area, where the police were noticeably missing, the Minister continued to sit in the car watching intently as the men broke the windows of the vehicles ahead, pulling out shivering, frightened people, administering their version of justice with their weapons.

Then Manu ran his fingers through his hair, smoothing it down as though before a television audience and told Harlal to pull over by the side of the road. Rafat had broken into a sweat and his mind had flitted like a fruit fly on a bowl of spoiled fruit, wondering how he could escape without alerting anyone. And with his very next thought had wondered if his job would wait for him if he did indeed give in to the impulse. The boys had bloodlust in their eyes and were close, too close.

Manu opened the car door and descended. He strode forward and raised his arms up, as though ready to embrace. Rafat reluctantly followed close behind. Then Manu's commanding voice drowned out the sounds of breaking glass. It was like listening to the hum of the wind before a storm. His tongue deployed words and lashed them like a whip dexterously undermining the youths' motives, discharging rationality with a tinge of violence. The police arrived on the scene just as the terror of the moment dissipated into an orgasmic calm.

Kanti Devi was the mother of Manu's three children. Dressed in starched cotton saris, her face and neck resembled a tortoise emerging from the depths of its rounded shell. Rafat wondered at the hold of a wife, any wife, but especially Kanti Devi, who vaguely smelt of ripe yellow melons. Rafat pinned it down to the voluptuousness of her contentment—neither predictably dreary nor annoyingly buoyant.

Kanti Devi left short notes around the house, clichés and banal phrases that hardly made sense. "The thing about abnormality," Kanti Devi wrote in a note she left on the coffee table in the living room, "is that there is no room for it in our lives."

At public appearances, Rafat stood silent and watchful behind Manu's white-maned head and tightly sculpted face, waving his MSJ embossed fan for all to see, shooing away blowflies, bottle flies, fruit flies, houseflies, grain flies, sewer flies, animal flies and robber flies. In private, Rafat became Manu's factotum, part of the back engine of the Ministry, dealing with the media, organizing meetings, preparing agendas and planning out Manu's personal vacations.

Rafat reasoned that it was probably his own imagination. Manu was caged behind the barriers of a predictable marriage and conventional affairs. Increasingly, he registered awareness in Manu's glances.

Over the years, Rafat convinced himself that he was successfully insulated from the pull of his own desire. A desire that he feared as much as craved. Other than one late night encounter with a drunk college student who had initiated it yet had no recollection of it afterwards, Rafat had never acted on his urges. Even that one incident had expanded in his head like a sponge, terrifying him with its uncertain consequences. For weeks after, he monitored his every cough and too frequently visited the local medical clinician who scoffed at his appearances and prescribed violently colored syrups in unlabeled bottles.

There were many who remarked on the beauty of the two men, when they stood alongside each other—Manu and Rafat. Rafat had been told many times that his height, square jaw, shock of thick, black hair and ready smile made him seem like one of those white-shoe-wearing, tight T-shirted, implausibly muscled Bollywood actors.

At a dinner, when Rafat introduced Manu to the audience as a "man whose sense of justice is incomparable," Manu rested his palm briefly on Rafat's neck, just shy of the collarbone. It was a benediction, maybe a caress, and Rafat's body opened in response.

"Handsome is as handsome does, but do we have other accomplishments?" read one of Kanti Devi's notes propped up near the water jug.

Manu's unpredictability had a potency that caught Rafat in a vise of longing. It was as though Manu's every cruelty was his most endearing virtue. It was a strange triumph watching each of Manu's emotional indiscretions. And when he conferred the benevolence of his affection, it was altogether a different high. The magnetism of Manu's moods vaporized Rafat. Like water sizzling on hot metal.

Manu asked Rafat to research and write a paper on the rights of the disabled. When Manu read the paper Rafat had put together after staying up all night, Manu tore it up and threw it into the food that had been laid out for the two German Shepherds in the front yard, without saying a word.

“There are pills for all sorts of ailments, none for the ones that affect your conscience.” Kanti Devi left the note on a message pad by the telephone.

Harlal was driving Manu and Rafat to Gandhi Maidan where Manu was to deliver a speech on the twin evils of corruption and bribery. Just as they passed by some huts, a young child, about six years old, ran across the road directly in the path of Manu’s car. Harlal applied his brakes unsparingly. The brakes made a squealing noise sucking up and swallowing the little girl’s death rattle. The noise attracted people out of the huts and when Rafat got out of the car, the girl lay motionless on the mud road and there was already a crowd at the scene. Harlal backed the car and parked it a few feet away from the crowd. Then, before Rafat realized what was happening, Harlal opened the car door and took to his heels. Some of the men from the crowd gave quick chase and before long Harlal was caught and delivered to the angry crowd, who had by then realized that the little girl had died on impact.

The mother of the little girl appeared scared, confused and desperate. She tried to revive her child. Then in an act of utter defiance, she ripped the sari from her own chest, exposing her thinly clad breasts, as though she needed to display her own beating heart. The skin on her chest creased like crumpled voile. Two older women tried to drape the sari back over the woman's skinny chest.

Rafat watched this tug of war with the removed gaze of someone who was caught in the grip of an unbearably luminous moment. He got out of the car and approached the body. The little girl lay with her knees bent to one side. One hand lay curled and bent by her face. The other was outstretched above her head. The undersides of her tiny bare feet were dry, lined and dirty. It looked like the map of India. There was a gash on her forehead and blood was trickling out. Rafat saw the glint of metal in the dead child's closed fist. Rafat looked at his own hands and he was still clutching his Fly Swatter's fan tightly. Mechanically he began to flap the wind around the child's face, swatting at the flies that had begun to smell death.

The boys and men poured out from neighboring huts and descended on Harlal, engulfing him. No one heard Rafat's pleadings to leave the poor man alone. The sounds of the new violence reverberated and Rafat snapped his fan with meticulous purpose.

It was later, much later, that Rafat turned back to look at the car and realized that Manu was still seated in the front seat of his black sedan. He had not moved. Throughout, he had sat, still, staring straight ahead, cocooned within his space.

As Rafat approached the car, the passenger window cracked open an inch.

"Ek Color-TV deyydo," Manu instructed and the window rolled back up.

At the mention of "color TV," the weeping mother looked up cradling her daughter's dead body. Her eyes had blood flecks and blue veins.

"Sony? Trinitron?" the recently bereaved father asked, looking down.

The mother gathered her daughter into her arms and walked away with her sari pallu trailing behind her. Her labored steps pounded out the story of her inconsequence.

Manu's speech that day was rousing, passionate and blazed with urgency. Manu leaned too close, towards Rafat, his breath conveying quick excitement. Rafat felt as though he was reaching for something just out of his stretch. Rafat gathered together a memorial in his head and incinerated the incident of the little girl's death.

Rafat felt a sense of purpose in Manu's company. He waved his fan determinedly, the movement originating in the middle of his torso. The menace of this heave and pitch was not lost on Manu's visitors. Like every other political party, there was backbiting and influence peddling among party officials, especially during election time. It was apparent that the party needed Manu just as he needed the party.

"Life is an endless series of tests; some pass, some fail." Found taped to the guest bathroom mirror.

The more idiosyncratic Manu appeared the more the voters liked him. When Manu turned forty-three, he celebrated his birthday by distributing 100 rupee notes to the entire slum of Bird Bagicha, inhabited by hawkers, laborers and vendors. They cheered him, lifted him up on their shoulders, and garlanded him, calling him their God. There was discussion of building a temple to Manu on the same land.

Then a month later, Manu gave the order to evacuate the very same slum and 247 families were instantly rendered homeless. The police were sent to raze the encampment that had been created out of landfill just fifteen years earlier. Rafat was dispatched to observe reactions and when he came back with tales of thatched roofs set ablaze and old men, pregnant women and children among the dispossessed, Manu raised his hands to God. "The vagaries of fortune," he declared, "sometimes you're up and sometimes you're brought down to the ground, *mitti*."

"A betrayal stings most when shrouded with esteem."

Kanti Devi's note was found on the shoe stand by the front door.

When the slum dwellers organized their own resistance and refused to leave Bird Bagicha, Manu sent Rafat to negotiate. Laborers, cobblers and vegetable sellers raged about the injustice, when the wealthy were occupying the other part of the very same Bird Bagicha and nothing was being done to evict them. Weren't they encroaching too? It was because the rich had given money to these corrupt ministers.

After Rafat came back with his report, Manu switched tack once again. This time Manu took up cudgels for "these poor downtrodden men, crushed under the yoke of corruption." He presented himself in his all-white garb, called the media and appeared like a shining knight in white armor amidst the dirty, bedraggled lot complaining of their plight.

In the middle of a crowded room Rafat would feel Manu looking directly at him. It would be just a brief moment of connection—and the rest of Rafat's day would be powered by that one moment. Rafat found no escape from the haze of pent up desire, and believed he alone understood each one of Manu's whimsies. The media was not so sparing and heaped criticism on the wifflewaffle, with one *Indian Express* journalist going so far as to call him Manic Manu.

Kanti Devi identified the traitor behind the Bird Bagicha debacle as "the one you mistakenly trust, the one whom you believe is closest to you."

A story often told is likely to be believed and Kanti Devi's words began to acquire the shimmer of truth. Rafat saw it in her smile.

Late on a rainless monsoon day, after all the visitors had left the house, Kanti Devi had retired for the night, and the servants had been instructed to go to bed, Rafat prepared to leave. He began to shut the windows in the living room facing out into the garden.

"The clasp on this window looks loose," Rafat told Manu.

He then pulled the drapes closed and turned off the lights. He was preparing to put on his shoes lying near the entry doorway when he heard Manu approach. Before he could turn he felt Manu's hands slide up his arms to his shoulders. Rafat stood stock still, frozen as he felt Manu's fingers pressing down on his shoulders. Manu said nothing and Rafat tried his best to level each serrated breath. Then Manu's fingers slid over Rafat's shoulders onto his chest and then down to his ribcage. Rafat closed his eyes to heighten the sensation, the intoxication of those slender, ministering fingers. He heard the rising excitement of Manu's exhalation. Rafat turned to Manu in the darkened room. His knees buckled and he slowly slid to his knees in front of Manu.

Afterwards, when Rafat left, Manu held the door open for him.

"Goodnight," Manu whispered softly.

That night Rafat couldn't sleep, despite being bone-tired. Then just before dawn his breathing relaxed and steadied.

In the morning Rafat dressed carefully, choosing black as the color to offset his mood, tamp down his exhilaration. After a quick jolt of coffee he walked along Anne Marg to clear his head. With a sudden odd pang, he wanted to apologize to Kanti Devi. "Manu" he said aloud, adding "Rafat," softly tasting the names on his lips. Last night's indulgence filled his head. Rafat exulted.

When he arrived at Manu's front gates, Deepak, the guard, saluted him and then uncharacteristically came and stood in front of Rafat, blocking his way.

"Deepak?" Rafat questioned.

"Sir, you cannot go inside."

"What? Why?"

"Orders from Minister Sahib and Madam."

“What? I think there’s been a mistake.”

Deepak shook his head looking down.

There was a sudden lull in the traffic outside Manu’s house. Then it restarted. The world seemed to be in collusion. Rafat turned and stepped away, carefully drawing his gaze away from Deepak. A sweeper across the street swept the dust and the wind blew it towards Rafat. He coughed. His hands felt loose, lifeless. He shook it free. The fan flew out of his hold and landed on the ground, opening out and displaying its raised gold emboss.

The Blue Arc

The day Shona moved into Brothel No. 27 she also learned how to snip an umbilical cord. You attach two clothespins to clamp the cord and holding the cord firmly in your left hand, apply the sharpened scissors with deliberate force close to the baby's belly and in between the two clamps. Then gather the placenta and remaining umbilical cord and throw both into the street trash and hope that the stray dogs will find it before the crows.

She had arrived late morning with her red embroidered cloth bag that she'd bought at the Kalighat Hawker's Market last year. The bag held one *salwar kameez*, two white bras, one black bra, three frilled drawers, Ponds powder, kohl liner, red lipstick, black comb, toothbrush, Colgate toothpaste, a tongue scraper, a notebook and a photograph. The notebook was hidden in a secret pocket that she had sewn into the bottom of the bag and the photograph was tucked into the notebook. The notebook at the bottom of the bag made the base of the bag heavy, flat and rectangular.

As soon as the painted green door to No. 27 opened, Shona knew that the house was in a crisis of sorts. Without any greeting, a young girl wearing a long skirt and chemise, with eyebrows that met thick and strong in the middle of her brow, led her straight down a narrow, dark corridor to a room at the back. There were two cots in the room separated by a curtain gathered together and tied back with a purple ribbon. Two women bent over one of the cots on which a woman lay puffy and pregnant. Her legs were bent and her dirty white underskirt had been pulled off her strangely skinny legs. Shona's eyes were drawn to the curtain again, which seemed like the back of a third woman. Ma was sitting cross-legged on the only chair the room, issuing rapid commands to the girls. She continuously picked at and peeled the nail to her big toe on her left foot as she directed the women.

Shona recognized Ma, because Ma had chosen her out of all the other girls that had lined up for inspection at Sonagachi Brothel No. 21. Shona had been glad to leave that last place, where her bed had been in the middle of a corridor with curtains on two sides. Reema, her neighbor on the left, had lice, and day and night she could hear the incessant scratching. Shona had even invested in a bottle of oil that had set her back fourteen *rupees*, which promised wonders with lice. But the scratching had continued.

A few years ago, Shona had been happy to move into Brothel No. 21, which had been a step up from renting a bed for eight rupees a night, and sub-renting it to other whores, with no pimp for protection. Space was a premium in Sonagachi.

Shona stood to one side of the room clutching her red embroidered cloth bag to her chest. The women assisting at the birth looked to be older than her. Shona had heard a customer once mention that an average life span of a whore was forty. She still had fifteen years more.

The room was like any back room in any brothel, plain and unadorned except for a framed picture of Goddess Durga, which hung on the far wall above the light switch. This was Shona's favorite Durga image. The Goddess was seated on a lion holding ten weapons in her ten hands. The hands were in motion and looked like spinning spokes in a giant wheel. The longer she looked at the picture, the more it seemed as though the trident was in motion, descending towards the pleading, terrified figure of the male demon, Mahishasura. The goddess had a red glow to her. As a child, Shona had wondered if the redness was because of her anger, bloodlust, holiness or passion?

The laboring woman groaned and Ma's voice commanded authoritatively, "Push! Meena. We don't have all day. Customers will soon arrive; all your screaming will send them running next door." One of the girls standing by the bed placed her hands on Meena's distended belly and pressed down. Meena groaned loudly and pushed. On the fifth cycle of instructions, a baby popped out of the woman. Shona vaguely glimpsed its dark body.

"Hey, you!" Shona looked at the seated figure of Ma.

"Upstairs in the terrace room there's a medical student. Bring him down. This one needs to be cleaned up. Go on. Hurry. The least he can do is help out, renting the room for next to nothing." Ma looked aggrieved.

Shona held her bag and ran out. She looked for the stairs that would take her upstairs and couldn't find any inside the house. The solemn-eyed girl who'd let her in was twirling in front of a dirty, chipped full-length mirror in the dark corridor. Shona saw herself reflected in the mirror—dark faced, sharp nosed, narrow eyed and thin bodied. She looked at the child in the mirror. She must be about twelve years old. Her wildly printed long skirt flew out as she twirled. There was a dreamy look on this brothel-born child's face. It was funny how life was filled with such moments.

"How do I get to the terrace room, *Munni*?" Shona asked.

The girl continued to twirl and pointed to the front door. Outside, Shona found a spiral staircase hidden at the side of the building. She climbed all the way to the top and emerged into open, endless sky. The sun shone like a friendly relative. Irresistibly, she held out her arms and twirled like the child. The cloth bag fell to the ground with a thud as she spun around and around. She felt disoriented when she stopped. The door to one side of the stairwell opened. Shona's head was still spinning as she looked up at the medical student. He was of medium height, yet still taller than her, with a wide receding forehead.

"Can I help you?" His eyes bulged a bit and he looked intense.

"Ma ... Madam, wants you downstairs. A girl just gave birth to a baby. She needs help."

"Are you ... ?"

"Yes, I'm Shona ... new girl downstairs."

He nodded, "I'm Shiva."

There was no judgment in his manner. No doubt, he was used to people like her, thought Shona, since he rented a room in a brothel. She wondered if he was a customer too. He looked like a clean-cut boy from a good family, barely past his youth. How did he end up living in a brothel? None of her business, Shona shook her head.

They walked downstairs with Shiva leading the way.

Shiva greeted the child who let them in, "How are you, Kakoli?"

Kakoli giggled at the question.

Shona observed how Shiva stiffened at the sight of the woman who lay on the bed with the baby lying naked and slimy between her legs. "The baby is out," Shiva said obviously.

Shona laid her bag against the wall, and made her way to the bed. She looked at the baby and pointed to the cord that was still attached to the baby. She took the pair of scissors from the three-legged stool by the bed and proceeded to cut through the cartilage.

That evening, Ma put Shona to work and the baby took his last breath.

Shona liked No. 27. There were fewer girls—only six of them and then there were Kakoli and Mishra, one a whore-in-waiting and the other a pimp-in waiting. Ma kept a close eye on the business. There was something about Ma that reminded her of her own mother.

Most particularly, Shona felt kinship with Rabindranath Tagore, the resident pimp, bodyguard and escort. Upon being told his name, Shona knew immediately that Rabindranath Tagore was of different stock, not like the brutish, drug trading pimps she was used to. First off, he must be from a good family for otherwise he wouldn't be named after India's literary hero. And then, which salt-loving man would carry around a name like Rabindranath Tagore without it seeping into him in some indefinable way? Ma had mentioned that he was nimble footed in avoiding trouble that came in the form of police, patrons, peddlers and pillagers. Shona came to the conclusion that Rabindranath Tagore's story was possibly worse than hers.

She had an unwritten rule, never to talk about her circumstances and never to ask about others. Sympathy was like an incurable disease.

Rabindranath Tagore and Shona struck up a cagey relationship. Shona was polite and obedient and always, always backed him, even when she knew he was lying. On his part, Rabindranath Tagore reciprocated with suspicion and wariness. Shona made sure to call him by his full name each time she addressed him. That was her attempt to remind him of who he really was.

Ma was a progressive brothel owner. She provided condoms to customers and she had a third year student at Calcutta Medical College check the girls periodically. Not Shiva upstairs, who was still in his first year.

The month that Shona arrived, Ma joined the Durbar Mahila Samanwaya Committee (DMSC). She explained to the girls that the committee was like a union for prostitutes. The other girls didn't really understand what a union was. Shona explained it by saying that they wouldn't have to bribe the police as much. Ma also talked often about how the girls were nothing but slaves, sex slaves, and the government needed to stop this exploitation. Shona marveled at that, for really wasn't it Ma who was the slave mistress then?

About four months after Ma became an active member of DMSC, three policemen arrived at No. 27 just before sunset. Rabindranath Tagore led them into the dimly lit waiting room, deferentially indicating the girls standing there. The policemen were laughing and smiling as they walked in. Shona looked at the men and knew.

"Get your madam." It was an order. Kakoli went running to obey.

Ma bustled in. She had on her face her most obsequious smile, the smile that she reserved for the police, rich customers, and the local thugs who demanded money from her periodically. "How can I help you gentlemen?"

One of the policemen had his lower lip peeled out exposing the vulnerable pink inside. He looked at each of the girls standing expectantly—Rupa, Munira, Bina, Kamala and Shona. He was bald and his uniform stretched around his middle. He rocked gently on the heels of his feet. His eyes swung back and connected with Shona's. He walked up to her and licked the tip of his pinkie and caressed her cheek with that spit-dampened finger. Shona felt the wetness and lowered her eyes. Her cheek throbbed. The policeman turned abruptly and walked up to Rabindranath Tagore. Looking at the pimp, he asked, "How have you had the temerity to join Durbar Mahila Samanwaya Committee?" There was no threat in the voice or manner. It was almost gently posed.

Rabindranath Tagore folded his palms. "No sir, I didn't. Honest, sir. I didn't. I wouldn't do that. That's a women's organization, isn't it?"

The policeman turned his head to look at his friends and imitated Rabindranath Tagore's tone, "Isn't it?"

One of them smiled, then chuckled and then began to laugh. The other joined in and they laughed and laughed and laughed. Shona could make out spirals of tension rising like loose powder from a compact.

Ma didn't say a word.

The policeman unbuckled his belt slowly. Shona ran forward. One of the other policemen grabbed her and twisted her hands behind her back. "Come to me, my little pigeon," he said and he flexed his free hand in front of her. His palm was enormous and his fingers short and stubby. He extended those fingers and squeezed her left breast painfully. She closed her eyes and for the next few unbearable minutes every cry, every plea, every groan from Rabindranath Tagore seemed to issue forth from her own throat.

When she felt her hands released, she knew it was finally over. It was an unbelievably hot day. The heat shimmered from everything: the chair, the bed, and the walls. Shona went to him as he lay on the floor and touched his cheek. He was still alive. The breath came out hot and then hotter from his open mouth.

Later that evening, she grabbed her red embroidered bag and ran outside and up the stairs. She sat against the wall and hugged her knees. The bag hurt her but she rocked side-to-side holding herself in. She emptied her mind, like she'd taught herself, and then reached into her bag. She painstakingly undid the seams to the hidden pocket and took out the notebook and opened it. She stared at the double lined page which had words written densely together in a beautiful flowing hand. She remembered her father writing in the notebook. She turned the pages. It fell open to the words.

And the cracked shell

Of lingering grief

Rolls along

Gathering doubt and disbelief

And the blue arc

Dances in delight;

You are in me

That is my plight

This is my complete.

She passed her hands over the inked pages, tracing each letter, each word.

She closed her eyes. She forced herself to feel that blue arc.

Shona remembered so clearly her father's hands, hanging by his sides, loose and disjointed, the day they had ceased to be part of his complete; his right hand with the mole near the thumb as he wrote in the diary, and his left hand holding down the top of the page; and again his hands, stained white with chalk dust, as they swarmed over the blackboard. Shona couldn't remember his face as clearly as those hands.

She turned the pages of the diary and could feel the photograph even before she reached it. She didn't need to really see it, she told herself. But she took the photograph out. There they were, the three of them, captured in black and white, confined within twenty inches of rectangular space; her mother smiling prettily, happily at the camera, the red *bindi* on her forehead accentuating her glowing eyes; her father, dressed in his schoolteacher clothes, black pants and white shirt, looking solemn and serious. Shona had been twelve years old in the picture, Kakoli's age. Her two long braids were looped up on either side of her face. Her eyes looked eagerly out. Shona couldn't bear to look at herself.

Shona placed the photograph back inside the double lined pages and put the diary away. The secret pocket at the bottom of the red embroidered bag needed sewing again.

Ma didn't attend the DMSC meetings again.

After the beating Rabindranath Tagore dropped a cerecloth over his real character. Sensitivity was so out of place in his world. He had no choice but to change. Shona did her best to keep to herself and away from his crossness and his flying hands and fists. That resolve was tested the day he brought to No. 27 a young girl, barely fourteen. Shona saw herself in the child, for hadn't she started on this path when she'd been fifteen? The girl held her tears and terror frozen in the overlarge black pupils of her eyes. They looked out at the world as though from a distance.

"Clean her up and dress her. Her name is Madhu. She can start today."

Ma smiled.

"Where did you find her?" Shona asked.

"At the railway station," Rabindranath Tagore replied. "She was weeping because she was abandoned. I told her that we would take care of her," he looked pleased at his good fortune. His teeth looked startlingly white in his brown face.

"Does she know where she is?" Shona persisted.

He shrugged. "Who cares? You?"

Shona did care, but she held her tongue. She looked at the girl. Had she followed any part of the conversation? If she had, there was no indication on her face. She wasn't a great beauty, which was certainly an asset in the trade, for otherwise she would have been overworked. She was dressed in a bright pink skirt that reached mid calf and a yellow blouse. Her breasts and hips looked as though they had some growing left. Her tightly braided hair was looped up on either side of her face, just like Shona's had been in the picture.

Shona took Madhu inside.

"Do you know anyone in the city?" she asked.

Madhu shook her head.

"Do you know where you are?" she asked.

The girl lifted her eyes and looked at Shona. Her eyes flickered and there was an instant of awareness. Shona stopped questioning her. It was better for the girl to continue in her shutdown state. Survival took many forms.

She went to Ma and asked her to give the girl some time.

Ma refused, saying, "These things are best done right away." Ma told Rabindranath Tagore about Shona's request. Shona learned that evening what it cost to defy the pimp.

With the rains dousing the streets and flooding the potholes, business slowed. Shona, dressed in her faded blue modest salwar kameez, walked out of the house toward the bus stop carrying an old umbrella as protection against the rain. She boarded the first bus. The conductor came to her and she said in her most cultured tone, "Alipore—National Library."

"What do you want with Alipore? You stick to Sonagachi," he said with a smirk.

She faded inside. She wanted to ask, "How did you know? Is it written on me? Where is it written? What makes you better than me? My father was a schoolteacher and I can recite Tagore's verses in

Bengali and English. Can you?" But she didn't utter a word and her silence was the price she paid.

The rain paused and a weak sun began to shine as she got off at Alipore. She sat on the bench facing the National Library, conscious that she was gauzily apparent. She spent two hours on that wet bench, watching people come and go out of the library. In the past few months, she'd come once a week to the same spot and the same bench and had yet to find the courage to go in. She closed her eyes. One day, she told herself, one day she would find herself inside browsing the shelves, probably on another rainy day just like this one.

When she got home that evening, it was late. She'd had to change two buses and walk a couple of kilometers. Rabindranath Tagore was waiting for her.

"Where did you go?" he asked

"To Alipore," she said, adding lightly, "Did you miss me?"

The anger on Rabindranath Tagore's face dissolved and he said mildly, "When you leave the house, let me know where you're going, and don't take so long. We don't run a charity here." The knuckles on his hand stood out as he talked and Shona nodded, thankful she didn't have to explain.

There was a protest march led by DMSC. It started at midnight with women and children holding banners demanding social rights for sex workers. Shona watched them and heard Ma complain about how this was a waste of time and income, for customers were scarce. Hadn't Ma joined DMSC at one time? Was this a way to rationalize her withdrawal? Shona looked at the women marching and she mentally put herself there in the midst of the group. She opened her mouth and repeated the chant, "We demand equal rights. Remove the Immoral Traffic Prevention Act. Ours is a profession just like any other. We want respect." She watched as a woman about her own age, dressed in a sari with her evening makeup on, danced along the street and moved her hips to every word chanted. She turned her face and her eyes met Shona's. The woman's eyes were shining and alive, and her hands were upraised, swirling, creating small quick circles in the air. It looked as though she was drawing little goodness halos. There was purpose on her face. This woman had probably measured her life with the many faces of her customers and yet found the inspiration to raise her hands. Looking at the happiness on the woman's face made Shona feel unutterably sad.

The procession and the chanting lasted for about an hour. When they left, it seemed as though a crater had been dug in Sonagachi. The place looked lonely and desolate. The echoes of the protesters' chants still reverberated through the street. Shona turned to go into the house and bumped into Shiva who'd been standing silently behind her. Shona apologized and stepped back. He shook his head and smiled at her. The emotions under control broke and a sob escaped her parted lips. Immediately, Shiva's round eyes filled with concern. "Are you ok?" She nodded her head and kept her lips pressed tightly together and went running in. Through one corner of the window that faced the street, she saw Shiva look back at the house and slowly climb the stairs to his own room.

Kakoli was becoming a woman. Ma saw it, Kakoli's mother, Rupa, saw it, and Shona saw it. Her smile had become coquettish and her walk was attracting notice. She left the top two buttons of her blouse open one evening and Rupa slapped her. She wore a sullen look as often as she wore a flirtatious look. It was time, thought Shona.

The day that Rabindranath Tagore saw it was the day that Kakoli entered the profession. Her prized virginity was sold for seventy-five rupees and Ma acquired another whore. Kakoli's eagerness dimmed a bit, but then, inexplicably, she became more childlike, more temperamental. With Kakoli now in the profession there were eight of them making money for Ma.

Winter was approaching and Shona felt the urge to go to the terrace and smell the oncoming chill. She picked a time when she knew Shiva had classes, and she climbed the stairs. Up on the terrace, she took out her father's notebook but couldn't open it. She sat in the corner and gazed at the gray sky. She held in her hands the only tie that bound her, she thought. The diary was a burden she carried.

She dozed a bit and woke up to find her open notebook in Shiva's hands. He was standing and staring down at her. She leapt up and grabbed it from him and stuffed it into her bag. Her hands were slippery as she pushed the book in.

"English Poetry?" he asked, the puzzlement mirrored in his eyes.

She gathered herself and ran downstairs ashamed at what Shiva had seen. For the first time in a long while Shona felt exposed and vulnerable.

That night she deliberately rushed through the landscape of her past, like she was in a train watching each scene flash by. Her father, the English teacher at the Manimala Girls School, talking about the poet laureate Rabindranath Tagore and Kazi Nazrul Islam and Michael Madhusudhan Dutt; Shona with her best friend Seema at school, surreptitiously reading a pulp paperback; their house, two rooms and a kitchen, clean, and well kept; the Government Hospital where mother was diagnosed with cancer; Father's worried face; Father coming home with money, enough to pay the hospital bills; Mother's painful death, despite the money; the moneylender demanding his money back; Father selling everything there was to sell, jewelry, sofa, chair, books, clothes pots, pans; the moneylender giving Father an ultimatum; a knock on the door; Father being hit over and over again; Father's glasses breaking into shards; Father's eyes seeping as Shona is raped; Father's suicide by hanging and then Shona bewildered and alone. The story was used and old.

The next day, she trekked to the air-conditioned office of the Durbar Mahila Samanwaya Committee. She had to bribe several committee members before she was allowed to register herself as a sex-worker. Shona didn't mind that at all. Bribing was a trade like any other trade. Champa Devi, the social worker at the office, asked her to put her thumbprint down on the registration form. Shona signed her name.

Shona was given the task of putting out flyers in Sonagachi. She applied herself diligently to the task. She kept her bundle of flyers and sticky tape in her red embroidered bag and as she walked to the teashop or bus stop, she would furtively tape her flyer alongside all the other flyers. She went to fancy nightclubs on Park Street and stuck flyers on the walls and on telephone poles. She handed them to street vendors. She even put some outside The National Library.

Champa Devi was pleased when Shona went back for more flyers.

On her way back from the DMSC office, Shona exulted at the weight of the new flyers in her bag. It seemed like the weight of a baby in her belly. At the bus stop she paused when she saw a familiar round face. Shiva stood there cracking his knuckles, as he waited for the same bus that she would take. His fingers were long and slender. Grey and white pigeon droppings defaced the striped red and yellow cement enclosure. It seemed so right, to see him there.

On the bus, they stood close to each other and Shiva's dry palm touched hers. She opened her palm and his hand slid comfortably around hers. They didn't talk or look at each other. They fell into step when they disembarked from the bus and walked to No. 27 together, without touching.

"Why do you go to Alipore every week?"

Shona wanted to ask, how do you know, have you seen me, who told you, but this was Sonagachi a teeming town where everyone nevertheless knew the whereabouts of everyone else. That thought gave Shona pause. For did that mean that everyone in No. 27 knew about her joining the DMSC?

"I go to The National Library," she said. There was no point in hiding it. "I don't go in," she rushed to explain,

"Just sit outside."

"Why don't you go in?"

Shona stayed quiet. She didn't know the answer to that.

"Are you scared to go in?" Shiva asked.

Shona shook her head and then nodded, "Not scared exactly, just not ready..." she let her voice taper without finishing the thought.

"I can take you when you're ready."

"We'll see."

Shona imagined what it would be like to walk into the grand library, with Shiva as her escort; her long fingered book pimp. She smiled.

Inside the house, Shona saw Ma's eyes sliding to her bulky red embroidered bag and then looking away. The next morning, out of the blue, Ma's eyes filled with tears and she told Shona that they were all one family at No. 27 and they had to watch out for each other. Through thick and thin, Ma said, punctuating each word with a nod. Ma then requested that Shona go to the medical shop for ointment to treat vaginal boils.

"Here, take this money for the medicine. It's for Kakoli. Poor child. Barely four months in the business."

Confused and moved by Ma's concern, Shona took the money and walked to the store. Shona tried to connect Ma's words as she walked. Ma wasn't sentimental generally, so what was this about? Was it because Kakoli was so young? Shona supposed they were family, for they did reside together and cooked and ate together and they were jealous of each other like siblings and took care of each other's illnesses.

When she came back with the ointment for Kakoli Shona felt warmed by her own thoughts. She hurried in and found Ma, Rabindranath Tagore and Mishra standing clustered together near the coal stove. They turned and looked at her as she stood in the doorway. Ma's face was sorrowful. Rabindranath Tagore's eyebrows formed two hooks over his nose and Mishra smiled. Shona's eyes shifted to the stove and she saw her red embroidered cloth bag on the stove, on fire. Shona watched riveted at the sight of the red bag and the red flames. She could make out the DMSC flyers curling into the flames. The notebook at the base crackled and the bag split to reveal the burning double lined pages. She thought she even saw a quick glimpse of her black and white photograph. Shona saw her father's face above the fire: nose, eyes, mouth and lips, all fusing into his face.

She stood conscious of being watched and realized that the story of her past was being abbreviated. It consisted only of her memories, those that she chose to keep. Shona felt light and free. The future, she thought, the future still stretched ahead. Calmly she smiled at Ma and handed her the ointment.

The next day, she waited outside Shiva's room. When he came up the stairs, she announced, "I'm ready."

Mustard Seeds

Fire is like a Fibonacci sequence. It spirals into infinity, if left unchecked. It's a function of fate, a sequence of life. F(n) = F(n-1) + F(n-2) ...

It was in the ninth grade that Mrs. Saxena taught me all about Fibonacci sequences. My desk was on the far side of the window and my imagination on the stiletto of sunlight that shone on part of the sequence on the blackboard, illuminating it. 0, 1, 1, 2, 3, 5, 8, 13, 21, 34, 55, 89, 143, 232 ... The number thirteen had stood out limned by light and shadow. Oddly, it was the only one of the sequence written on the board that was made up of more than one digit and the digits didn't repeat or contain successive numerals. I was thirteen when I fell in love for the first time. I remember her clearly. Maya. Her large eyes would fall on me in class and the words would disappear from my tongue. I would sit there with my hand raised and my eyes visualizing our joined sequence. The first time she talked to me, I felt a physical ache more powerful than what is about to happen to me.

Will she remember me? Will she reconstruct our interactions?

"*Jaan*, I knew this man. He used to be crazy in love with me at one time. Hahaha. What a joke it was. You'll never believe it. He asked me to marry him, when we were fifteen. His was my first proposal. I hope they don't come around looking for me because I knew him in high school. Will they? Oh my God. What do we do?"

Or it might go, "Why are they doing this? This was a good man. He asked me to marry him when we were teenagers. He was a little insane. Crazy insane. I could have loved him though. Do you know how and why they caught him? I cannot bear to think about it. This weekend can we go to the beach?"

The day I proposed to Maya was the day that Rao told me the story of the fire in a warehouse in Kashmir. The winter cold had formed icicles around the warehouse and an untended *kangdi* had resulted in a raging fire. Fire and Ice. The pictures were breathtaking, Rao had said. The cold icicles holding form despite the heat from the burning building. Maya was the fire that would melt my icicle. With a rare burst of resolve, I went looking for her. I found her just as she was about to enter the restroom in school. I called her name and she turned to look, her long earrings swinging like tribal dancers. There was impatience on her face. I dove to my knees in front of her and grabbed her hand.

"Will you?" I asked.

"What?"

"Will you...marry me?" I whispered

"Let me go."

"Not until you give me an answer."

"Is this your idea of a joke? Are you making fun of me?" she responded indignantly.

"No joke, Maya. We'll marry when we're eighteen."

"Let go of my hand. I need to go to the bathroom."

I remember clutching her hand tighter and her face wincing and then her great burst of rage, swinging her fist at the back of my head, my falling forwards and her clutching her groin as she violently freed herself and ran into the bathroom crying.

As the skin fries off my bones, will I be dead already?

Asphyxiation is what kills; I know this because of my friend Rao's fascination with fire. I remember when I was eleven and Rao had struck a match and watched as it crept slowly down to his thumb and forefinger. Then just as it reached his skin he threw it on the ground and lit the next one. The second time, I saw the fire touch his flesh and I yelped in distress. He smiled at me and threw the match down.

"Nothing will happen," he assured me. "Watch one last time. The fire will die down on its own." He struck the third match and I watched as it lit his thumb a full 10 seconds before he pinched it dead. Rao showed me his thumb and forefinger. There was proof that this was not the first time he'd done this. "The fire will first attack the nerves and kill it. After that you won't feel anything. Try it!" he told me. "If you're ever trapped in a burning building, more than likely it will be the smoke that will kill you. It's like drowning," he explained. Instead, I was burned by the encounter.

I know the smell of burning flesh.

It is a smell that comes to me when I think of train compartments full of people sealed and set afire and widows forced to enter the funeral pyre of their dead husbands and people trapped in burning buildings waiting for rescue and Tamil rebels in Sri Lanka tied to trees with tires hung around their necks and set aflame. I am not a Tamil rebel. I am a man born to a Religion and a Country. My mother is my Country and my father my Religion. Both have let me down. I wait here today, my eyes covered by a strip of gunnysack, waiting for flames to devour me. My captor smells of something visceral. Of sweat, cigarette smoke and polyester. Funny thing about polyester is that it is highly flammable. How ironical. I feel my condemned mouth stretching.

I think the fire will be ignited around me. The floor will be covered with straw, and gasoline will be liberally poured around me. It will need just a single match. The flames will rise slowly first warming my feet. It will seem like a mere walk on hot coals. Then it will rise. First attacking the nerves on my feet. Quickly devouring my shins and broken kneecaps. The flames will attack my anus, my digestive tract and the lining of my lungs. I will then lose consciousness. At last I will be consumed by eternal peace.

When the police came for me, it was half-past one in the morning.

"Traitor," they yelled, shoving me and pushing me. "People like you don't deserve to live."

I watched my sister weep, begging for mercy. "Don't hurt him, don't hurt him."

I heard my fourteen-year-old brother, his stutter loading the mirth on the men's faces.

They mocked him and imitated him, while I lay supine at their feet and my sister's voice reached madness.

"S-S-S-St-Sto-Stop i-i-i-i-t," they said before slapping her and grabbing her breasts.

I met my brother's eyes and pointed with my chin. He walked across the room to assist my sister. There they stood, a silent, scared rag tag army of two.

I got to my feet, dragging their attention back to me.

In a few violent seconds I was on the floor again. From the floor I looked at my siblings, commanding them to stay still and unresponsive, without the words ever being said.

I was dragged out and pushed into a waiting car.

Carbon monoxide, they say, is odorless; it is so much easier to deal with an unsuspecting killer.

I recall movies I've seen, where the killer creeps into the heroine's room with a knife. She is usually sleeping oblivious to the deafening sonata of suspense. Then she wakes up, just as the hero appears clumsily, noisily, and captures the silent killer, while the heroine completes her wakeup routine, wiping the sleep off her mysteriously unsuspecting face clad in a black or red or white negligee and looking with exaggerated horror into the face of what might have been. My eyes are sealed shut to my might-have-been.

In these few moments awaiting my pyre, I have never been freer.

We are tied to a goal, an ideal, a motive or desire that pulverizes the idea of freedom. Yet, there is a constant struggle to find that elusive sense of abandon. The fleeting moments rarely add up to a sustained perception of liberation. In my life, liberty was measured out like tonic. In small, spare doses.

The past tense seems very apt here, for the future is just a thought away.

When I was told about the death of my journalist father, who died in prison after a year of incarceration, the sense of relief that overwhelmed me was my moment of *freedom*. *Freedom* was when my fragile, beautiful mother killed herself. She had tumbled into the pewter pits of melancholy and depression and couldn't see her way out. Or when my sister broke off her love affair and returned to us. Or when my brother got a scholarship for the coveted computer science program of a well-known university. Or when I joined the outlawed party of the people. *Freedom* was a word, a concept that we talked about when we met. But we were bound by the very act of desiring *freedom*.

Is that the sound of music I hear?

As a youth, I'd heard about the rock star rebels who'd created music and sold it under the shallow guise of art. It was passion and politics that had pulled me into their record banner. In my careless naivete, I assumed that the lyrics of nationalism and courage would shield the anagrams of combat and conflict hidden in the songs.

But, the government spoke the same language we did. They solved our anagrams, parsed our rhetoric and deciphered our allegorical references. They threatened us with obey, adhere, respond and surrender.

Yet, I played my violin to the rebel drumbeat. I played in alleyways, in coffee shops, in college libraries and in private homes. With the rage of past injustices thrumming inside me, I played to stray dogs, and old ladies, and babies in bassinets, and brothers and sisters and teachers, and vegetable sellers. I forgot about the price I would have to pay. The music I hear today is nothing like the angry rhythm I am used to. It is soft and melodic and heralds the coming of my angels.

Each flame will rise up a little higher, curling at the very tip like a batik pattern across space.

The baby was in discomfort, her breathing painfully labored as I laid her beside Gajra on the narrow bed. The afternoon sun reflected the brown batik pattern of Gajra's sheet onto her translucent skin, and it seemed as though the child's entire body glowed from within. The fire was inside her body. I looked down at the mother and child on the bed and exhaled loudly willing my breath to cut across their thresholds. My wife and my child. That night the fragile child recovered but the mother died giving up her battle easily, peacefully. Wrenched by the prospect of a life without Gajra, I left my child behind.

It had been at my cousin S's wedding that I finally

muscled up the courage to approach Gajra, my future wife. I had seen her around town. She worked at a restaurant, waiting on tables. I made it a point to visit the restaurant once a week. She never once acknowledged me, never indicated that she recognized me or even that she knew what my order was going to be.

"What would you like to eat?" she'd ask each time, with the same inflection of assumed obliviousness.

"Breadbutterjamandtea," I'd say, all in one breath.

Each time, she laboriously wrote it all out in her little pad.

At the wedding, I watched her stride toward the buffet table, marveling at the fact that she was the tallest woman there, almost three inches taller than me. She loaded her plate with food and then she stood in a corner by the trash, and proceeded to remove the mustard seeds from her plate with a fork. Dip, pick, trash.

"Why do mustard seeds bother you?" I asked as I threw my cigarette butt into the trash.

She cast a quick glance at me, laughed loudly, and continued on with her task. Dip, pick, trash. "They're food spies. Like mustard gas, they infiltrate and destroy."

"It's not as though you can taste them."

"Then what value do they serve?" she asked meeting my eyes.

In one smooth swoop, she dumped her whole plate in the trash.

"Let's go get something to eat," she said, pulling me by the hand.

"I want to sing," she said, later that evening, her voice lilting and tilting each word into a tune, and I didn't know whether she wanted me to know that because she'd heard of my music.

She finally sang at our wedding.

She put words to my violin.

Six months later, she was pregnant and in prison. She survived prison but died in childbirth. I played my violin at her funeral.

And then the flames will engulf, crackling and dancing in the inferno.

I danced for the first time as a young boy when my father received an award for fearless journalism. Those were the days when writing an expose meant ceaseless effort and endless praise. My mother had not stopped smiling. I'd worn a black suit and red tie to the event and watched my father rise up higher than anyone else. My last memory of my father was of a man whose body had rotted away in the damp of prison walls. Even after he died of pneumonia, pamphlets of his writing still found their way to street corners. I collected them assiduously and created a folder titling it, “My Prison, My Future.”

My sister is on the path to losing her future. I’ve seen her striated arms. When confronted, she denies it, and then remonstrates, “How could you think that of me?” I suspect that it is the hand of the government, feeding her narcotics to control her.

My brother’s stammer is worse these days. Last week I patiently waited for him to finish, “Fuck You, you, you, you, you are the won, won, won, won ... one that is the cau-cau-cau-cau-use of all our troub-troub-troub-troub-troub-troubles. I wish you would go away.” I asked him if our sister was on drugs and he told me to let her be. Later he apologized.

I lost my day job as a welder in an auto parts factory. My boss told me that I was on the government watch list and the company would lose its license if they continued to employ me. I withdrew all my savings and left it in the My Prison, My Future folder.

Dip, Pick, Trash.

I hear the sound of a footfall. There is excitement.

"We have good news for you," a voice announces.

I shift from one foot to the other.

"We've decided to let you go."

I stay quiet. I can smell my sweat.

"Did you hear me?" a strident demand. "We've decided to let you go!"

A hand clutches my polyester shirt.

"Yes, you're going to be free!" Another ebullient voice.

I hear the sound of a striking match.

Strapped for Time

He held the handle of the safety razor and stared into his face in the mirror. The familiar feel of the razor handle in his hand calmed him. With his thumb he felt the smooth band in the neck of the razor. It was equably flat, unresponsive, smooth. He rolled his thumb down the handle and felt the wider band of embossed ridges; the friction created heat, which quickly shot through his thumb down his arm to his chest. He felt his breathing quicken.

This could be the moment, he thought. But after a minute of indecison, he smiled and applied the razor to his face. It was a safety razor that he'd bought in 1973. The years had marked a few nicks and he comfortingly felt them as the razor blade lay against his skin. The cold stainless steel blade was unremitting. A drop of blood appeared near the line of his chin and as he continued imperturbably shaving, he saw the drop grow larger and larger, providing a splash of color against the brown, lined face in the mirror.

He stood against the white porcelain sink discolored

with the hard water that came through the rusted pipes and peered into the small partially cracked mirror while washing his face. It was a mirror that had hung on the wall at the exact same spot for 23 years. The familiar cobweb hung like a piece of lace from the upper right edge of the mirror and swung to the wall in a graceful arch. The plastic frame was a gaudy gold which showed the strains of age. His weak eyes peered into the mirror and he could make out the cloudiness that ringed his pupils. Dr. Susheel had been persuading him to get his cataracts fixed but he held steadfast to his theory that all doctors were hacks, and he wasn't about to let any modern hack take a knife to him. So here he was, peering into a cracked mirror staring into his clouded irises. What a word, iris! Why would they name a part of the eye after a flower, he wondered? Which came first, the human eye or the flower?

After he finished shaving, he patted his cheeks with exactly two drops of Old Spice. No more, no less, for it was his treasured bottle. He'd had it for over eight years now. It was now down to half. He carefully capped the bottle, closed it tight, and rinsed and wiped clean his razor and shaving brush. Then he walked to the wooden cupboard near the window. He placed everything back in its place on a newspaper sheet that had been spread on the shelf. The newspaper was dated April 1993. There were large yellowing stains on the newspaper and the edges had started to curl up. But he was loath to replace it. Change was an unwelcome intrusion into his life and often accompanied a harrowing period of adjustment.

He walked back into the bathroom and started the water, which fell with a loud splash into the orange bucket that lay directly under the faucet. He took off his *lungi,* undershirt and boxers, just as the water filled almost to the brim of the bucket. The timing was perfect. As he peeled off his boxers and dropped it into a red round shallow plastic tub, the water was almost ready to spill over. His lips cracked open as he chortled in exultation at the perfection of his timing. Then he leaned forward and poured that first pink plastic mug of water over his body. It was bitterly cold. Despite bracing for the water, the cold knife like chill of the water made him shiver involuntarily. The second mugful was always the hardest. There was absolute certainty in that second pour.

He sat down for his morning prayers. The sun probed a hesitant entrance into the room. He threw open the window and the golden light rushed in to prostrate before the nine small pictures of Gods and Goddesses that decorated the wall of his altar. He had one much-worn book of *slokas* lying to the side and he picked up the book and commenced to read from it. His voice rose and fell in a lilting tone that he'd heard uttered in his own childhood. His tone soothed and consoled him as he read and chanted. He looked into the face of each of the idols displayed on the wall and he felt connected to his own existence. There had to be a greater reason, he assured himself.

When he was done, the ornate ormolu clock on top of the television read ten minutes after seven in the morning. The clock was a gift from his old British boss, Brandon F. Bradley. It was gold-plated and had the figure of a cherub playing the violin. He remembered Bradley's words as he'd handed it to him. "For your loyalty to the company, Mr. Raman." He'd, of course, elongated the second 'a' in his name. Thirty-two years he'd worked for the man. This was his reward. His mispronounced name and an ormolu clock. The clock was his prized possession, he reasoned, as he went into the kitchen to prepare a glass of coffee. Painstakingly, and with sparing use of a spoon, he measured and mixed. Sometimes, he preferred to use the *handle* of the spoon to stir. It was just an ingrained sense of thrift. He took his cup and seated himself at his post, an upright chair that faced the television and the door. He took a loud slurp of the coffee and turned the television to the news channel. His body began to ready itself in anticipation.

The hands of the clock inched its way towards eight. Eight-o-five. She is late, he thought. His terrible need for the doorbell to ring made him restless and he shifted uncomfortably as he stared at the door. He muted the sound on the television. The loud second hand ticking of the clock seemed like explosions.

Why was she late? She'd begun to do this very frequently. She knew he waited for her. It was careful, premeditated callousness. His body elongated and he sat straighter in his chair. His mind emptied and he focused on the door. His glasses began to slip down his nose and he slowly pushed them back. A vein on his neck throbbed. The minutes moved on lazily and the breeze from the open window wafted into the room gathering fleeing particles of dust on the floor into a round swirling transitory ball. He watched as the rolling mass splintered into fragments that settled on top of the chair, the television and the rectangular coffee table.

The doorbell rang stridently and he got up and opened the door. She walked in nonchalantly, handing him the newspaper that had lain outside the door. "You're late," he said calmly. There was no hint of the agonized anticipation he'd suffered. He shut the door and watched as she walked with a saucy twitch to her behind. She turned around and looked at him and said flirtatiously, "Were you waiting for me? Poor old man!" But there was a mocking glint in her eyes. He stood there at the door watching her walk towards the kitchen. She came back out and met his eyes.

"What?" she asked, belligerently.

"Don't come late tomorrow. Look at the time, it's almost 8:30," he said softly. She tossed her head in response. Sometimes I will and sometimes I won't. I have other things to take care of in the mornings. You can find someone else who'll come exactly at eight." Pause. "Or you can buy me a nice wrist watch."

There was a derisive twist to her lips. She commenced dusting while he unfolded the newspaper and turned off the television. There was comfort in the sounds and smell of a human body around him. The warmth engulfed him and he felt cocooned in the sweep of a tender emotion.

"Ok," he said, "I'll get you a watch."

She looked at him startled. There was a quick flash of something close to sympathy in her eyes. It was just that one brief moment of intimacy and it branded itself on his chest. He felt inclined to forgive her for everything else. Circumstances had made her what she was and greed was essential to her survival. Her next words gave truth to that thought. "A good one, like Titan," she said, adding, "And I like the ones with the gold strap, okay? None of the cheap silver for me or the black leather ones; No, Grandpa, it's got to be gold." Avariciousness had become another terribly exciting, rough facet of her character.

For the rest of the one hundred and thirty-five minutes she spent in his house, her steps had a jaunty spring to them. She even sang when she washed his boxers. At one point, she heard him coughing and with the insouciance of someone who's probably seen it all announced, "Now, don't wet your underpants, grandpa. You know how I hate to feel your wet boxers." He squirmed in embarrassment and his face filled with color. She laughed raucously.

As she swept the floor, her sari pallu slipped off her shoulders and he was treated to a voluptuous display of overflowing flesh that would stay with him for the rest of the day. He swallowed and tried to avert his eyes but they were pulled inexorably towards the laughing, snide figure that knelt suggestively on the floor by his knees. He glanced at the clock, willing it to slow down. His eyes followed her while she knelt, bent, stood, twirled and performed any number of gyrations that soothed and solicited. When she disappeared into the kitchen to wash dishes, his head slowly descended to his chest in exhaustion. He was rudely shaken awake when she was done with her chores.

"Why don't you go sleep inside, old man?" she asked.

"Because you might rob my house from under me," he said jokingly, but both of them knew that it was no joke. She just might.

She shrugged in response. "Ok, I'll see you tomorrow.

Now, mind you, Titan with a gold strap." She wagged her finger in his face.

There was an earthy, musty smell about her, an unwashed essence that titillated his senses. He breathed her in and silently watched as she left, shutting the door behind her. Emptiness reigned in the small apartment. He sat in his chair, with the newspaper in his hands and his glasses on his nose, wishing for the next day. As the hands of the clock advanced, he began to diligently go through the various sections of the newspaper.

Then finally he came to the section that he denied himself till the very end: *The Obituaries*. He took his little notepad out and began writing a list of all the people featured in the section. There were nine people listed. He wrote down the ages of each one: 85, 82, 86, 62, 72, 76, 59, 87, and 87.

He himself had just turned eighty-one. It had been a birthday that no one had remembered. He had secretly celebrated on his own. He had bought a small cake and a candle. Before her arrival, and after his prayers, he'd blown out the candle and sung just the first line of "Happy Birthday," in a gritty self-conscious voice. He had felt so furtive about the celebration that he'd made sure he'd closed the open windows and turned off the lights so no one could have seen inside. Then when she arrived he had offered her a piece of the cake, saying that a neighbor had brought it over. She had taken the proffered dessert happily and finished it in front of him. As she licked her full lips, he'd felt overcome. Now, as he reflected on his birthday, he felt a sense of guilty joy.

He counted five people who were older than him from the newspaper's Obituaries. Five out of nine: that was more than half. He sat back satisfied. He wondered what he'd do if there were more people younger than him who died?

In the afternoon, he stood at his second floor balcony and watched the school children come home. He watched as the cows munched on refuse lying alongside the street. He watched an altercation develop between two teashop customers. He watched the local city bus unload a group of people.

No one ever looked up.

Patiently, he stood there waiting for someone, anyone to notice him. It was as though he had already ceased to exist. When his watch indicated the appropriate hour, he painstakingly put on his outside clothes and open-toed sandals and stepped out for his daily walk.

He wended his way down the same street he'd spent an hour watching, but as he passed his apartment building he paused and with a very definite movement of his head, looked up at his empty balcony. There was no one there, of course, but he felt better for having done that.

Later, back in his apartment, he went to his bedroom and pulled out the padlocked iron trunk stored under his bed. He unlocked the trunk and surveyed the contents. They were his deceased wife's belongings. There were eight silk saris, some necklaces and bangles, an unopened perfume bottle and there it was, all the way to the back of the trunk, a little Titan box. He opened the cover and sitting in glorious arrogance was a wristwatch that he'd seen his wife treasure and wear infrequently. It had a gold strap. A wave of nostalgia flooded him and he sat there looking at it. Was this betrayal, he wondered? Then with determination he took the little box out and re-padlocked the trunk and painstakingly pushed the trunk back so it fell back to within the same dust free shape on the floor. It took a bit of maneuvering before he got it just right.

At nine p.m., he obeyed routine and dutifully laid his head down on the pillow. But it was as though someone was holding his eyelids open, for he couldn't fall asleep, yet he felt the need to yawn continuously. He shifted from one side to the next and determinedly kept his eyes closed. He imagined her face with his eyes closed, her round, dark eyes waiting eagerly for him.

In the morning, he waited for her. When the little hand on the clock swung to the eleventh digit, his heart raced in anticipation. He looked at the slim shape of the watch box. He caressed it and his eyes watered. He looked at the calligraphed letters on the gilt case. The last two letters had faded a bit and his eyes could only make out the first three. "T-I-T." He reached for his glasses but couldn't find them. "T-I-T," it said staring boldly at him. He closed his eyes. The laughter burst from him. He said it aloud, "Tit" and then said it again and again. He laughed so hard that his chest began to hurt.

By eight-thirty, an overwhelming sense of disappointment assailed him. She was late again. Did she not remember? If she only knew what was waiting for her, he thought. Resignation and then despair soon followed.

It was around nine forty-five when the doorbell rang. His chest still hurt. Laughter was not good for him, he thought. He walked to the door and opened it. A woman stood outside. Her friend or sister, he wasn't sure. This woman had worked at his house a few times, he remembered. He looked at her. Her eyes looked puffy and swollen.

"Rekha died last night. After she left your house. Hit by a car. Right outside your balcony." The woman began to wail loudly. His chest pain intensified and he could barely stand there holding the door open. "Right outside your balcony, at eleven 'o clock."

He'd been reading the obituaries at the time.

He wanted this stranger gone. "Do you want me to clean your house?" she asked. The tears continued to pour down her face.

Clutching his chest, he shook his head and pushed the weeping woman out of the way and slammed the door shut. He slid the bolt home and then staggered to his chair. It seemed like a slow fire had become a raging inferno inside his chest. It was becoming hard to breathe. Slowly, he reached for his pen and pulled out the familiar notebook. The page was open and had the following numbers freshly written: 83, 48, 78, 91, 81, 54, 69 and 88. At the end of the list he added 36.

Curtains Drawn

"I am like a mango tree!" Da exclaims. His arms spread wide and his fingers extend out. I look down for that familiar crooked jagged line at the left corner edge of the floor. The curtain's floral pattern is reflected on the floor. The flower petals look diffused and the edges are distorted. I look back up at my father, he is still smiling and his arms are still outstretched, like a giving mango tree. He stands there looking for approval and reluctantly I respond, bobbing my head up and down slightly. His hands come down and he turns. As though through a mirrored reflection, I can see his face as he walks away, the smile broad and beautiful.

Outside, I feel blinded by the light. I can hear my father's laughter loud and clear from inside the house. I look around and hear other sounds. The sound of the school bus idling, Auntie Keya's German shepherd barking, four-year-old twins, Maya and Mala, banging steel pans in rhythm to a nursery rhyme, Dr. Ghosh's car starting up. The multicolored memory of last night fades to sepia.

"Da," I say when he comes out dressed for work. "Look, that bird."

"What about it?"

"I think it's bruised. It's not able to hop. There, do you see it? It's dragging."

"Survival of the fittest, son. If it cannot survive ..." he shrugs and leaves the words unsaid. He gets into the car and drives off with a wave, missing the dragging sparrow by a few inches.

I walk up to the bird. The eyes are perfect circles, anticipating and fearing my intervention. I reach a hand out and quickly grab it before it can move away. The bird's chest heaves in terror. I caress it, rubbing my index finger down its feathered back. It feels soft and hard. The heaving subsides, but the eyes still move restlessly looking for rescue. "Trust me." I whisper to the sparrow.

I look back at my house, hesitating about going in. The house is like every other house on the street. Whitewashed with a dark teak wood front door and white window trims. The windows that face out to the street have curtains that protect our secrets.

I remember walking down that same street last week, late, after the lights in every house had turned out the day. At Dr. Ghosh's house, there are no curtains and I'd stood watching, that evening, as Dr. and Mrs. Ghosh weaved in and out of their living room. I heard my mother call my name but I had not wanted to leave my spot. Dr. Ghosh had reached for a newspaper and I had angled my head to make out the words, *The Statesman*, while he'd held the newspaper extended in both hands. Then he'd neatly folded the newspaper four times. Reaching for a pencil from a table nearby he'd written something in. I knew it must be the crossword for Mrs. Ghosh once told my mother that he'd won the title "Crossword Fiend" during his residency at Calcutta Medical College. Mrs. Ghosh had walked in and peered over her husband's shoulder. She'd pointed at something on the folded newspaper. A clue? Dr. Ghosh had nodded and smiled, bundling affection in that stretch of lips. That smile pierced me as I'd stood outside in the dark. The faint sound of music had wafted out, like the powdered glass string of a kite. Not anything familiar, songs sung in a different tongue. It stung.

I walk into my house with my injured bird. My mother is in the kitchen. She turns and looks sideways at me. My heart beats painfully and the bird shifts in my palm. I'm thankful I cannot see the other side of her face, immediately. She glances at the bird and meets my eyes. She goes and gets an old dishrag and a cardboard box. She motions for me to put the bird down. I put the bird in the box. It stares up at me with shallow eyes and then looks down. There is no depth to the bird's eyes; the whites have overpowered the brown pupils. My mother gets a large sieve and places it over the box. The sieve is round and the box is square. This misalignment bothers me.

Breakfast is set out and I pick up the fork and slowly deliberately mash my peeled, hardboiled egg till it is a mess of white and yellow. I eat in silence without taking my eyes off the trapped bird. I can smell my mother. She stands behind me. She smells of cloves and fatigue. Her hands reach out to place another toast on my plate. I look at her hands, brown and veined. The veins are ridges of blue on the back of her hand, the skin hardly masking the color.

"What do you want in your lunchbox?" she asks

I shrug. "A fruit, whatever."

"That's not enough."

"It is. It's just about bloody enough." I yell and leave the house.

In the evening, I pull myself back into the house. It is clean and smells of seeds. Coriander, Fennel, Cumin, Pepper and Poppy. Seeds of sadness. Yesterday's decaying odor still permeates.

When Da arrives, I'm at the dining table with my

books spread out and my mother in the kitchen. She comes out, when she hears the door, and for the first time in two days I look at her face. The shame overwhelms me and I quickly look down.

"At your books, son?" Da asks in his loud buoyant tone.

I nod my head, with my face determinedly down.

"Do you see that, Su? Our son doesn't have the time to even look at his old man. Children these days! What has my beautiful wife been up to all day? I smell something, delicious. Do you smell the food, Vik?" my father asks me. "Your mother's spent her day slaving for us. Have you thanked her, huh?"

Obediently, I look at my mother and the words come out a little more forcefully than I expect. "Thank you, Ma."

"You don't need to thank me," my mother says, "Thank-yous are for strangers."

I wish I understood her, her quiet, her forbearance, and her rejection of my thank you. Oddly, I feel hurt. I then remember my bird. "Where's she? Where's my sparrow?"

My mother points to the kitchen and I run in. The bird is sitting in the box, still alive, with her chest gently dipping in and out. The eyes are dull, though, as though her fight is close to over.

"Ma, did you feed her?"

She comes into the kitchen, and says softly, "Yes, Vikram, sunflower seeds and some bread crumbs. I peer into the box and the seeds and bread lie strewn, untouched."

"She hasn't eaten it." There is a plea in my voice.

My father comes into the kitchen.

"What is this? What is this?"

"The bird," I say.

He looks at the brown box and shakes his head disapprovingly. "Son, nature has its own rules. The brave die proud, the weak are the ones who suffer. Let this creature out of its misery." My mother stands beside me and her hand on my shoulder tightens. "For him," she says.

"Draw the curtains in the living room," Da commands abruptly after a few moments of silence. "Do you want everybody to look in?"

I take my sparrow and go to Dr. Ghosh's house.

"Can you take a look, Sir? I picked her up this morning. Something's wrong. She almost got run over. She hasn't eaten all day."

Dr. Ghosh ushers me in and I stand against the

window as the surgeon flexes his fingers and wiggles them. Then he shakes them and finally, gently, beautifully picks up my little bird and examines the bird's beak, legs, stomach and chest. Then he says, "I'm not a bird doctor, Vikram, but it looks to me like the left leg is broken and she needs a splint." He goes to the kitchen and comes out with a matchbox. He fashions a splint with two match sticks.

I take the bird back to my house. The curtained house creaks with quiet. I creep into my room with the bird in the box.

The next day Da is cheerful and animated. He takes me to the movies and talks to me of having courage. I laugh at his jokes and feel light and undone. There is freedom in this. So I laugh louder. My father's answering laugh is like a gunshot, booming and bursting.

These are the days in between. It seems irrevocable, this happiness. By the third day, even my mother has relaxed enough to smile at Da. His cheerfulness is like a disease spreading and striking. Da pulls my mother to him. She stands in his embrace, looking at me. Da releases her and comes to me, running his right hand over my hair. He asks about my bird and looks into my precious box, and marvels at Dr. Ghosh's splint.

Happiness and shame, I reflect, are related. Both are to be hidden; both cannot be displayed. My mother has figured this out already. She begrudgingly accepts happiness and readily accepts shame. I am shamed by my happiness.

Behind the drawn curtains, Da and I solve quadratic equations and parse French grammar. My mother keeps us fed and hydrated as we wrestle and rollick foolishly. She is never a part of it. She stands behind an invisible line and watches, silently. And in her face there is a waiting.

Then, on the fifth day, Da brings home his misery. He is the same man, I reason. My mother looks into his eyes and knows the pattern of the next few hours. I watch as her face empties. The emotions slowly drain from her face; sadness, concern, happiness, hope and yet still acceptance. She goes through the house and draws the curtains closed in every room. I am trapped inside.

It is later, when I need to fill the bird's bowl with water, I venture to the kitchen passing by the dining table where Da sits sprawled with a glass of amber in front of him and a lit cigarette resting on the ashtray. He sees me and beckons. I approach and he sees the bird in the box. He reaches inside and takes the bird out. Then he laughs. In a dirty minute, he's reached for his own box of matches and lit one of them. While the live bird sits within his grip, he applies the match to the splint. The bird goes up in flames.

"There! I've solved your problem!"

My mother lunges at the flaming bird and Da applies his fist to her almost healed upper lip. It splits again.

Da wakes up around noon. I'm waiting for him.

His Curls

As I lie registering the last convulsions of a contracting pelvis, the doctor holds him out to me. He is covered in blood. I shake with the force of the after effects and the unsightly view of my son. His tiny mouth opens and he executes a perfectly piercing scream that grows from the depths of his tiny naked abdomen to his dilating chest to his face and open mouth. There are parts of me clinging to his body and I shrink at the thought. This was what I had been waiting for, the arrival of my son. Here he is, the heir and keeper of our traditions. Would he be the strong, brave, kind human being that I envision? I gather my thoughts and blow them out with my next breath. This is my child! I bow to this destiny purposefully.

I am his mother and I dream of peace. Peace in my house, peace in the neighborhood, peace in the world.

His father whispers his name into his right ear. My child looks impassively back into his father's eyes. There is nothing there. No rush of emotion, no flicker of recognition, no indication of divine understanding. As I watch, his face screws up as though he cannot bear the scrutiny; the regard of all the eyes on him. He wails. The adults gathered in the room laugh at the inconsequentiality of his tears in the face of God's will.

Then he turns five. It is a wondrous year. He is my baby still. The curls on his head bear testimony to our bond. There doesn't seem to be anything else that likens him to me. I brush his curls with my fingers and sweep it away from his forehead, watching as it flops back in unruliness. Forever unruliness.

The newspaper headlines scream, "Colombo burns." That one line is set in bold type against the backdrop of a burning flame. The imagery of the burning headline stays in my memory for the rest of the year.

Civil war rages in Sri Lanka and as the world watches, the American Marine Corps Headquarters in Beirut is bombed and then the next year Indira Gandhi is shot dead. Riots erupt like pus out of an open wound. There is mayhem on many streets across the world. I continue to rock my baby gently to sleep, singing him lullabies that talk about a world we do not live in. He grows within the confines of my life and imagination. He plays with his cousins, sleeps in my room and laughs at my funny faces. I take pride in his normalcy.

"What is ass-ass-ination?" he asks me. His eight-year-old face is an earnest mask as he puzzles over the pronunciation of the word while asking the question. I debate about forbidding him from association with evil words like the one that was just uttered. Then think about the other words that have typically brought me down on any particular day: Carnage, terror, massacre, killing, and violence. I explain the meaning in simple terms. "It is the killing of an important person."

"Like Grandpa?" he asks.

I smile at him and shake my head. "No, not like your Grandpa. Olof Palme was the Prime Minister of Sweden and someone just shot him dead."

"With guns?"

"Yes, with guns"

"Like in the movies?"

"Yes, like in the movies."

"Bam, bam and the bad guy dies!"

"But in this case the good guy is supposed to have died."

I can see in my son's face that this is too troubling a concept to follow. So I just give up and watch as he exits the room excitedly at the thought of some villain dying.

Does he understand what assassination is?

When he turns ten, the hair on the back of his head has flattened and all the whorls have gone. There are just three waves on the top that are reminiscent of his baby curls. This is his only resemblance to me. But I know that I'm his mother. I do not need any external manifestation to reinforce that ... do I?

It is the year my son is introduced to religion. I console myself with the fact that he probably is too young to do anything with the knowledge. Every evening he sits in front of his father and grandfather and repeats parrot fashion what they explain to him: about life, about tolerance, about violence and about women.

Pan-Am flight 103 explodes over Scotland and Libyan terrorists are suspected. I can see the sky open up and shower a colorful sea of human debris.

In his twelfth year of existence, I discover semen stains on his bed sheets. Quietly I take the sheets and wash them. His boyhood has all but disappeared.

In Tiananmen Square hundreds of pro-democracy protesters are annihilated. As I read the newspaper, I can hear my son read aloud from the holy books. In Nicholas D. Kristof's report of the disastrous event, I read quietly, "Students said, however, that at least five hundred people may have been killed in the crackdown." That day, I think about what five hundred means. It could mean an entire neighborhood in a town or a small village. Who picks up the bodies after a carnage?

"Oh Lord, bring us forth and we will do right," says my son loudly and clearly. I look at him and can see the shapings of a young man. He sits still and serious, his jaw showing just the faintest undergrowth. Eruptions along his cheeks mark his age and his voice has begun to show a strain. A deepness that seeks to escape. I see a serious boy who is searching for an emotional place. I try to talk to him, but cannot; the words are trapped inside me. He has taken note of my limitations.

I begin to feed a stray cat that year, which is white in color. Despite the filth that he roams in, the white of his coat is a pleasure to my eyes. It's a murky white, but white it is nevertheless. It is the white of purity and innocence. Every morning I set out a little bowl of milk and watch as the white cat laps up the white milk. The two different shades of white seem vast oceans apart when placed side by side. Everyday the cat comes to me and allows me to pet him. I caress his belly while he purrs and tries to follow me indoors. I laughingly shut the door on his face and watch as he mewls plaintively sensing my presence behind the closed door. After a few minutes of scolding, he leaves. I then forget about him till the next morning rolls along, for my life is always thus compartmentalized.

One evening, at dinner, my son relates my friendship with the white cat with an indulgent smile. His father smites him across his face for showing an effeminate emotion. The force of the blow swivels his face to the left; towards me. My body jerks, but I say nothing. I watch as father and son glare at each other, one with irate careless disaffection, and the other with angry resentment. But that resentful glance suddenly turns towards me and I feel the full force of a trapped virulence. I am at fault.

Stubbornly, I continue to feed my cat. A week later I set the bowl of milk routinely outside and watch as it slops the sides of the bowl to fall on the ground. I call out to the cat, but there is no sign of it. The next day, the same thing happens and the next day. I feel perturbed at the unnecessary waste of good thick milk. Where could this fickle cat have gone? It is towards the end of the day that word is brought to me that a dead white cat was found in the alley by the Chinese restaurant. It had been slit open with a knife and its innards had been disemboweled. The nocturnal animals had got to it before it had been discovered and thrown away.

That night, I lie in bed wondering who the cat murderer is. Maybe ultimately I am the killer, for with my careless affection I had made the stray cat relax its guard. With breakfast the next morning I serve my son a question, “Do you know what happened to my white cat?” There is a calculating innocence in his eyes as he smiles and shakes his head in negation. “Why—has he stopped coming? Ha, ha, even a stray cat is fed up with your ministrations, mother!"

Life pursues us diligently for the next two years, providing a routine of escape and surrender throughout the day. I am just a passive observer in this drama that is my life. My son, on the other hand, has begun to need to believe. He believes in his strength, his defiance and in his faith.

The World Trade Center in Manhattan is bombed and the newspaper reports talk about the "face of death." Is it the face you wear when you are faced with death or the face you wear when you cause death? That night I dream of the face of death. It would probably be a face as dissimilar to mine as possible.

My son turns fifteen and there is just one tendril of hair on his head that curls rebelliously. I cling to that tendril of possession.

He looks at me pityingly most of the time. I don't have what he has—the youth and freedom to pursue his own dream. I ask him one day, "What do you want to be when you leave school, son?" My son isn't especially brilliant nor is he particularly foolish. As I wait for his answer, the significance of the question assumes a terrible importance. "A prison guard," he says smiling at me. The words boomerang within my head. A prison guard? I try to smile at him, but I feel the muscles on my face stiffen. I widen my mouth and bare my teeth. The bile rises as the dimples at the side of my face deepen. My son watches my reaction carefully.

At the end of his sixteenth year, he graduates from high school. He is at home most of the time. He wakes up mid-afternoon and eats through mountains of food. Then he puts on his outside clothes and walks out of the house. He comes back late in the evening and demands food again. I spend my time waiting for his disappearance and reappearance and dreading both.

Surliness writes its lines on his forehead and pinched mouth. He is still my child, just a teenager, I remind myself, and a sudden affection overtakes my reserve and I caress the top of his head. He shakes my hand off and glares at me.

In Rwanda, close to 800,000 people die at the hands of the Hutu militia. The event is officially named, a "genocide." The reports of the massacre filter through a few *Reuter's* news sources in the local newspapers, radio and television. The Hutu militias who wield fear and machetes in equal doses execute a brilliant game plan for extermination of the Tutsis. Hutu civilians are expected to kill their Tutsi neighbors or be killed. I exclaim at the horrific picture of a mutilated Tutsi woman whose arm is extended for help as she is being killed. My son comes over to look at the picture and then hands it back to me. In the next breath he asks me to find his missing shirt. I put the newspaper down and immediately get up to obey.

He is a man now, almost eighteen. His hair lies flat on his skull. I rarely see him smile. I offer him the newspaper in the morning, but he shakes his head and scoffs at me for reading "trash," as he calls it. "I can tell you without reading the newspapers what's going on in the world. Stop reading these propaganda printouts," he exhorts me.

His best friend stops by the house, one day, and asks me for my son's whereabouts. I have to admit I don't have a clue. I explain that he usually comes back later in the evening. That evening the two friends meet outside the house. A confrontation takes place. I watch nervously as they pummel each other. That is the day I notice the muscles on my son's arms. They stand out as he lifts his friend by his throat and flings him to the ground. I tremble at the calmness on my son's face. He comes into the house and tells his father he is moving out. My husband, his father, accepts the announcement with a cheery wave. I feel the weight of an unspoken revelation.

For one year, we see him sporadically. He comes into the house as though he's never left it. The familiarity of his footfall does not rouse any of us from our customary tasks. His reasons for coming are never questioned. He usually stays till dinnertime and then departs. Once he comes and stays through the night. I hear him yell out in his sleep. I count the hours till his departure.

I know that I love him still. He is my flesh and blood. In all my youthful imaginings I had always envisaged a son who would be the only one to understand me. Yet it seems like I am the only one who does not understand him.

It is my birthday in February and my son calls to tell me that he has a surprise for me. I am to accompany him to a crowded street market where he promises me that I will get what I dearly want. I wonder what it is that I dearly want. Revealing nothing more, he comes at the appointed time on my birthday and picks me up in a rented car. Why the splurge, I ask him. He indicates that he has come into a little money. I sit in the car wondering where he got the money from and how.

We drive to the market where I see throngs of shoppers in gaily-colored clothes looking for trinkets and scarves and mingling with locals who buy their weekly supply of fresh food and snacks. I smile at my son, glad to be amidst all the gaiety. He buys me clothes and my favorite dessert. He then asks me to follow him. "Here is where you need to wait, mother," he says and salutes me. We are on the second floor of a three-storey building, a good vantage point. "Don't move from here." I nod my head, expecting him to come back to pick me up.

I watch as he walks down the street. I can make out his tall, well-muscled black clad form. In the midst of the market, I lose sight of him for a short period and then I see him again. This time I watch as he stops and raises his fist in the air, shouting something I cannot hear. With a feeling of dread, I watch and wait. The crowds close in on him and I don't see him anymore. I remember stories of bomb blasts in the midst of crowded markets and I desperately search the crowd for him. Disobeying his express instruction to wait for him, I run down the stairs and into the street screaming for him to stop. People turn to look. I hear a burst, an explosion.

Excruciating pain and anger overtake me. I scream with my mouth open, unendingly. Someone comes to me and shakes me. I stare and repeat my son's name over and over. Hands lead me away. I walk with my eyes wide open, sightless. I search for the bodies and blood, the red fire, the body parts. I can hear the screams. It seems to me that there are people everywhere. I want to see my son's body. Will there be pieces left for identification?

As my eyes search the ground, a hand shakes my shoulder and I turn as the sound of a kitten wails shrilly with fear and despair, echoing my emotions. I turn and look up into his eyes. Mine are reflected in his, a river of sorrow. He stands before me, wearing the clothes he wore. I see the child that he is. He holds out his arms. I look down to see a little kitten nestled in the crook of his arm. I look up at his full head of hair with not a single curl.

Neyyappams

Ingredients: Rice flour, plain flour, jaggery, fresh coconut, bananas, cardamom powder, ghee, salt and water.

Sankar rose reluctantly from the warmth of his pallet and went to the window. He could make out the lone areca nut tree, its leaves waving like beckoning talons in the dim filtered moonlight.

He had been vigorously shaken awake a few minutes ago by his brother Kannan who had crawled back into the comfort of his bed soon after.

"Is it morning already?" Sankar had asked Kannan a little disorientedly.

"About midnight," Kannan had whispered impatiently. "I've been trying to wake you up for the last five minutes. Get up now. The baby was born at Eleven thirty-five. You've got to go and inform Vadyar that Amma's had a baby girl. Did you get that? Eleven thirty-five."

Sankar's father, Vadyar, worked at a temple across town. He groaned at the thought of the long walk ahead of him.

Sankar walked to the window and peered outside. The usually bustling street seemed painted into stillness. A faint light filtered through one of the downstairs windows and the verandah outside was just barely visible.

The incandescence of 30-watt bulbs had just replaced kerosene lanterns in their house. It had been a huge occasion when the neighborhood electrician, Murugan, who doubled as the town carpenter and plumber, had installed a wire and hammered a hook into the wall of each room in their home. Then he had deftly twirled the wire around the hook and plugged the switch into the socket located midway on the wall. The naked bulb had flooded the room with light.

For the occasion, Amma had fried *vadais* for the entire family. Murugan had eaten most of them while Sankar had surreptitiously counted the number of times the man had held out his plate for another helping. Every *vadai* that went to Murugan had been one less to share between him and his brothers. Murugan that night had set a record—eating seventeen *vadais*. With bones that tended to jut out of his rail thin frame, Murugan gave the impression of being undernourished and Amma had heaped the *vadais* on his plate.

Sankar and his younger brother, Kovil, slept on pallets placed close to each other on the floor. Kannan's pallet was further away and closer to the window. For a fleeting moment he wondered why he was the one who got picked to go across town in the middle of the night. The last two births had been during the day and Kovil had made the trek both times to deliver the news. Why was it his turn in the middle of the night?

This was his mother's sixth baby. Two of her children had died within the first week of their birth. Old Mrs. Nayar had assisted in all the births and deaths. Sankar had once heard the neighbor Mrs. Gowri remark on how Old Mrs. Nayar had assumed the position of Town Midwife by virtue of the fact that she had experienced eight pregnancies and six childbirths herself. With that impressive statistic, according to Mrs. Gowri, Old Mrs. Nayar had inadvertently found herself the official baby-deliverer for the entire town. At the last count, she had thirty-seven proud births to her credit. With this baby her tally would be up to thirty-eight. The last time he, Sankar, had made thirty-eight runs at cricket it had taken him close to three hours and some very bad bowlers.

Old Mrs. Nayar wasn't very old, but her face looked like a ruled notebook. She was a short rotund woman with a disproportionately large behind. As a result, she lumbered while walking, heaving her backside like a ship caught in a typhoon. Her torso flung itself into the fray with every sideways movement of her behind. Sankar often joined the jeering group of children that followed behind her, imitating her great sway. Sankar would watch as people smiled when she waddled by. Poor Old Mrs. Nayar if she realized it was sniggering rather than good humor, she never let it show. With a slight twinge of discomfort, Sankar remembered Mrs. Nayar's innocent smile on her round rulered face.

He made his way down. The house was not very large. Downstairs, there was the kitchen, one large hall separated into two rooms by a plastic curtain and one small room that was filled with a narrow, planked, wooden bed, two trunks filled with Amma's clothes and one carved teak box, a *kaalpetty*, which Amma had once told him she had brought with her from her girlhood home into her marital one. That room was never used for sleeping, except on the three days that Amma was segregated from household duties on account of her having "the curse," which event occurred with unbecoming regularity every month, except when she was pregnant with another baby.

He heard Mrs. Nayar in that "cursed room," as Sankar called it privately. He wondered if his mother would be able to get up and make dinner for them. If not there would be rice and milk from the family cow, Lakshmi, an inadequate offering that failed to quell his hunger for spices.

His stomach growled at the image of the soft puffy white *idlis* that his mother usually made for dinner and served with the angry colored *mulagapodi* that was freshly ground each day. The smell of the red chilies filled the air when his mother's bangled wrists rhythmically turned the pestle as she ground in the stone mortar. The tinkling of her bangles rose to a crescendo with each burst of speed that his mother threw into the grinding. The smell was thick and piquant. His eyes smarted and his throat thickened when he was close by. But the sound and the smell were irresistible, drawing him closer each time till his mother would catch him looking with tears rolling down his face.

The thought of the smell of the *mulagapodi* brought his gnawing hunger to the fore. He imagined a feast, an array of *vadais* and *idlis* with the thick red *mulagapodi* being served on his plate and the sesame oil being drizzled on top. He shook himself. It was the middle of the night and he was thinking of food.

He debated about putting on his walking slippers and decided that it would fray them since it was quite a distance away. He reverently put the slippers back on the stand and set out barefoot.

Their house was on the outskirts of Tripunithura

and Sankar had once heard George from the Lending Library remark on the lushness of the landscape. Since then he had looked at the eucalyptus, jacaranda, jackfruit and mango trees with that description rolling in his head.

Sankar passed by tall rubber trees that had sap oozing into a metal bucket tied to the thick trunk. The smell of sap was sickly sweet yet bitter, and overpowered the fragrance of the flowering foliage around—the golden showers and the jungle geraniums and the small white thumpa flowers. There were coconut trees right beside the rubber ones. When he'd been nine, Sankar had watched enviously as Kannan climbed one of those straight, tall trunks to pluck the coconuts that had been clustered at the helm. It gained his then eleven-year-old brother much praise and a break from the morning chores. Sankar hadn't conquered his fear of heights enough to attempt the task yet. One day, he promised himself.

In the distance, Sankar could make out the silent graveyard lying to the left of the road. There were no trees to act as sentinels against the wheezing creatures of the graveyard. As Sankar walked, the dread rose within him. He was told that there lived a ghost with a milk white face and a black body that disappeared into the night. The ghost came out when the sickle moon was up. The ghost crept from grave to grave looking for his dead child. He'd been warned by his friend Stupa who lived in the next street who was told by his mother's third cousin that if you saw the ghost he could disappear into your body, and your soul would then be inhabited by a disparate creature of the night. Sankar shuddered at the thought. He wondered if there was a sickle moon that night. Too scared to look up to verify, he kept his head down focused on each step he was taking. Through the corner of his eye he saw something approach and simultaneously heard and felt some movement. Throwing caution to the wind, he yowled surprisingly loud and high, anticipating his own ugly demise while running with his eyes tightly closed. A brutal hand touched his shoulder and clutched him hard. Cowering he covered his eyes with his hands.

"What's wrong with you?" Kannan's voice chided. "I called your name twice? Screeching like an owl, enough to wake the neighbors! Do you want to get us both in trouble?" Kannan glared at Sankar.

Sankar looked back at Kannan and admitted, "There are ghosts in the graveyard."

Kannan looked at the quiet, silent graves and laughed aloud saying, "I should have realized. Idiot! Amma asked me to give this to you. You need to hand it over to Vadyar and do not open it on the way," he cautioned. He handed over a packet wrapped in old newspaper and twine, "And don't loiter in the dark.

The ghosts from the graveyard will be watching yooooooooo!" Laughing to himself, he made his way back to the house.

Sankar clutched the packet close to his chest. He felt the warmth of his brother's body on the newspaper wrapping. He felt the package curiously. The contents felt round and squishy. There were blotches of oil stains on the newspaper covering. He put it to his face and inhaled the sweetness of sugar, the tanginess of cardamom, the smell of sweat, and the pungency of the newspaper. It gave him fortitude and he continued on.

Just past the graveyard were open fields. Sankar and Stupa played cricket with their friends at the north corner of the field after school most days and it looked reassuringly familiar. The field looked more grey than green at night. He continued on to the row of shops that lined the little center of the town. Starting with Balan's barbershop then came the cobbler, then the little post office with its red bell outside. The last store was Salim's Tailor Shop. On the other side of the street was the police station. Right beside that was Newspaperman Nair's house and then came the Lending Library. The shops were similar structures, with yellowing stained walls, brown doors with iron padlocks hanging like ornaments and large painted signs above.

Sankar glanced up into the sky to discover that it was a half moon. Looking up he kept walking and bumped into a telephone pole at the side of the street. At his brief exclamation of surprise and pain, the police station door opened and a deep gravelly voice asked for identification.

His head reeling from the knock, Sankar turned to look at Sir Thiru, the local Sub Inspector of Police. He was a portly man given to indulgent eating habits. Sankar had heard it said that Sir Thiru could eat three men's portions and still remain hungry. The local gossip claimed he was terrified of his little wife who was barely half his size but could reduce him to a puddle with just a slant of her sloe black eyes. But in the middle of the night he was a terrifying figure. His belly extended out and formed a shadow all of its own. His face with its long curling mustache seemed more a thug's than a policeman's. Sankar stepped into the light and announced, "It's I, Sir, Sankar. Amma has had another baby and I am going to get Vadyar to come home."

"Another baby, eh?" laughed Sir Thiru. "And won't be the last one, I think! On your way then son, and stay away from the fields."

"Yes Sir, I will," said Sankar respectfully and continued on.

His father worked in the Goddess Bhagavaty temple about five kilometers from home and slept there most nights. He was the temple priest and was paid by the royal family to perform religious ceremonies to keep monsters, demons, bad luck and bad fortune at bay.

Though his position depended largely on the goodwill of the townsfolk, his father considered himself an important personage. "I am the Vadyar of Bhagavaty temple," he was wont to utter and Sankar repeated the words quietly to himself, in Vadyar's imperious tone.

When Sankar reached the temple, he knocked on the ornate temple door. The door smelled of incense and sandalwood. After a few seconds, he heard shuffling footsteps in the inner recesses of the building and heard the lever being slid back to open. His father stood at the door, clad in a simple white undershirt and loose white veshti.

Vadyar of Bhagavaty temple, Sankar repeated silently. His father lived in one room at the back of the temple and worked two weeks at a time without break. Then he would come home for a four-day break before heading back to the temple for the next two weeks. This unrelenting schedule worked well for the whole family, for Sankar and his brothers would heave a sigh of relief when they saw him pick up his gunnysack filled with underwear, undershirts and veshti.

When his father was home, the sound of his voice could be heard down the street. While he was not a typically violent man, he had the temper of the devil and often a little incident would send him off into one of his tirades. More often than not it was when he or his brothers forgot a line of the Hindu slokas that his father made them recite morning and evening. Any mistake or hesitancy would be attended to in the typical manner. Father would give the boy five minutes to go outside and hand pick a branch from one of the trees. This would then be used with unsympathetic force on a trembling outstretched palm. It was usually Sankar who got the brunt of the stick and with a dexterity born of frequency he had learnt to twist his palm sideways in time to avoid the blow falling flat on his hand.

Filled with the anticipation of delivering good news, Sankar imagined his father smiling at him, that smile that lifted the corners of his lips and stretched them wide. Yes, he would smile when he realized Sankar had walked barefoot to give him the much anticipated news of a baby girl, the first girl in the family! The last time Kovil had gone, he had come back with the tale that his father had actually handed him some of the temple *prasadam* in addition to a pat on the back. He swallowed at the thought of the treat that awaited him.

Sankar stood at the temple door, holding the doorjamb. He looked at his father and said excitedly, "Vadyar, Vadyar…."

"Take your hand off, boy!"

"But Vadyar, Amma has had a baby…"

"DO NOT TOUCH THE TEMPLE!"

"... a baby girl!"

His father's face filled with rage and he swung his palm and gave Sankar a resounding slap! "How dare you," he cried! "How dare you!" Crack! Crack! His father's open palm delivered two blows in quick succession. Sankar's head fell back with the force of each strike. The carefully wrapped parcel that Kannan had given him fell. The twine snaking out trying to find its shape on the dusty moonlit floor. Sankar's eyes filled with tears that he tried to hold back as he stared aghast at his father's angry face and bloodshot eyes. He slowly took a step back and waited for the ringing in his ears to stop ...

His father's baleful glare wrapped around him and he took another step back. "You have despoiled the sanctity of this holy institution," he pronounced solemnly. "You should know that following the birth of a child there is a period of contamination, asaucham, for us. I am now unclean!" his father announced and gathering up the folds of his veshti, he stepped outside the doors of the temple and walked towards a small building at the back of the temple, ignoring Sankar who stood there with his mind blank with shock.

Sankar stared at the white columns ahead of him. Each individual frieze above the columns that flanked the door seemed to resemble a snake. The concrete floors outside the doors had a multitude of cracks on them, and there was an ancient bell that stood sentry in front of the door. Sankar looked at it all in a daze. His eyes fell on the newspaper wrapped parcel lying on the dusty floor. One side of the paper had ripped and he could see the sweet *neyyappams* gleaming like rich brown jewels, luminous within the dirty, stained and torn newspaper covering. As though driven by an unknown force, Sankar bent down and picked up the packet of *neyyappams* and popped one into his mouth. And then another and then another ...

He ate while he ran. The oil, the sugar, and the dust smooth and silky on his tongue. His feet began to throb. It had been a bad idea to leave home without those slippers. He could hardly see with his eyes cloudy with emotion. His face felt hot. He didn't want to think of what had just happened. Once the thought was outside of him it would never go back in. He was scared. He couldn't help it now. He just couldn't help it. The *neyyappams* were over and his feet hurt and his face felt hot.

Sankar, for the first time, felt the simplicity of hatred and the complication of guilt.

He was the middle child, reasoned Sankar. His younger brother was his mother's darling, and Kannan was the son and heir. Vadyar's son and heir. Grandmother Dried Lemon who lived close to Cochin called him the "mongrel-child." Grandmother meant well, but it chafed, nevertheless. Compared to his brothers, who had thick black hair, Sankar's hair was a mousy brown. When he turned eight, he heard some men talking at Balan's barber store about a black color that would keep the hair from showing grey. He wondered about it and often thought that if he ever earned money, he would buy the stain and remove all the ugly brown from his hair.

He ran as fast as he could, past the police station, Mr. Nair's house, the row of shops, the cricket field and the graveyard. The trees alongside the road looked like his father's hands reaching out to cuff him.

He kept running, his heart pounding and his chest bursting.

The Length of a Breath

The thing about an uncomfortable memory is that it has a tendency to get buried in the flotsam of life, under the shrapnel of everyday minutiae, of minor wrangling and major skirmishes. When it does surface, it presents a jagged edge, which, like the rocks over a rough sea, rarely persuade lingering or exploration. That was the case for Lizzie. She pushed the memory of her mother's death to some hidden chamber in her head and tried hard to immerse herself into the daily absorptions of her re-settled life with her uncle, Jose Ammavan. Yet, it showed up uncomfortably and awkwardly at inconvenient times.

Her preoccupation this year was mostly to do with her breasts. They had grown and grown and grown. Every few months, she'd had to request Jose Ammavan for money to buy a new blouse to wear with her long skirt. Jose Ammavan never noticed little details like bursting seams, ripped darts, or bulging flesh.

In desperation she'd even approached Mrs. Nayar, the midwife, in the hopes that the lady would have some remedy to stop her body from burgeoning any further. That kind lady had advised her to drink juice made with boiled anise seeds and to bind her breasts tight. She'd even loaned her the use of a thin towel for just this purpose. The next morning she'd bound her flesh so tight that she'd gasped for breath after every sentence.

The anise drink had been tolerable, at first, and then she'd developed such a gag reflex to the smell that she'd had no choice but to consider other options. After a month or so of binding her breasts Lizzie realized that her cleavage had begun to look wrinkly and seemed to extend closer to her neck. Furthermore, she'd seen two men near the toddy shop staring quite deliberately at the wrinkled cleavage. She released the binding and regretfully returned the garment to Mrs. Nayar.

The first time she approached her uncle, her mother's brother, she'd blushed a bit for the lie she was forced to tell. "Jose Ammavan," she addressed him, "I need money for some new blouses. All three blouses that I possess have holes and don't fit."

The next time, she approached him, Lizzie bluffed and deceived her way through the conversation: "Ammavan, you know the two blouses you gave me money to buy? They were of really poor quality. Look, they tore after two washes." Lizzie showed him two of the frayed blouses that she'd owned at first.

This now was the third time she had to bring up the same subject. She debated about using the same excuse as last time but Jose Ammavan was not stupid, nor was he forgetful, and he was more than likely to catch on, which would be the most humiliating experience.

That evening when Jose Ammavan walked into the house, his face was filled with tension. "Lizzie, there's news of a robbery and the police are everywhere. It's best to stay indoors. Who knows who'll end up becoming a scapegoat if these robbers are not caught. Where's Cherian?"

"He's outside with Zacharaiah and Pity Thomas."

"It's after dusk. It's not safe. Go get the boy home."

"Jose Ammavan, I have a request," she began hesitantly.

"Yes, yes, first go get your brother. The streets are not safe."

Lizzie found Cherian and Pity at the back of St. Mary's Forane Church. Both boys had four empty toddy bottles lined up and were trying to knock the bottles down with stones.

"Did you drink out of these?" she asked the boys.

"There was nothing there to start with," Pity replied.

"Did you put your mouth to the bottle, Pity?"

"I might have. What's that to you?" he responded belligerently.

"Wait till I tell Jose Ammavan about this. Then you'll know what's it to me. Cherian get up and come with me, Ammavan wants you home. Don't you have anything better to do Pity than to corrupt my brother? He's only eight years old."

Lizzie didn't trust Pity. Pity's father was always drunk in the evenings and Lizzie had heard that he beat his wife in his drunken rages. She knew that you couldn't really visit the sins of the father on the son, but nevertheless, she didn't trust Pity. She wished there were other decent boys for Cherian to play with.

"Where's Zacharaiah?"

"He's a goody two shoes and went home," sneered Pity.

"Something that you should have considered doing?" she retorted scornfully, her upper lip curling. "And you, Cherian, I thought you had more sense than to follow this stupid creature. That too behind Our Lady's Church. If you have to sin, couldn't you find a better place to do it?"

"Tomorrow we can drink toddy at my home, Cherian. How about that?" Pity laughed, revealing the gaps between his teeth. "Drink whole bottles of it instead of the drops left over in these used ones."

"Do you want to be a drunk like your father?" she shouted.

"Do you want to be a slut like your mother?" Pity retorted.

And thus quickly was the same memory resurrected. Everything in her life, good and bad somehow seemed inextricably linked to that memory. Pain and rage engulfed her and she saw the boy smile when he noticed the tears in her eyes. "How dare you," she said in a low menacing voice. "How dare you."

"My father says she was a ..."

Lizzie dove for the boy. She slapped his face and he grabbed her arms. Both of them fell to the ground and rolled. He punched her in her chest and the breath left her body. "Ooh look, she has breasts!" he mocked and his fingers clawed at her.

Lizzie lifted her knee and rammed it into the boy. It connected and Pity doubled over screaming in pain, yelling swear words in Malayalam that Lizzie had used in her own mind a time or two. She got up and grabbed hold of Cherian's hand. Cherian's face was wet. Lizzie refused to console him.

There was no escape. Just the other day, Jose

Ammavan had compared Lizzie to her mother. “You have her look. She was beautiful. So very beautiful,” he’d said, shaking his head.

She’d wanted to feel pride at the compliment, but had been saddened by Ammavan’s expression. She knew the gist of her mother’s story. She’d been too young when the scandal had taken place. Lizzie’s father had died of a heart attack just before Cherian’s birth.

Her mother had always been a cheerful person, but she had changed after Lizzie’s father had passed away. Lizzie remembered how frozen she’d been at her dad’s funeral. She recalled the village ladies urging, cajoling, even begging her mother to express her sorrow, but she had stood there with her features packed together. In fact, Lizzie couldn’t remember an occasion when her mother had ever cried for her father.

After her father’s death, her mother had moved into Jose Ammavan’s house where Cherian had been born. Jose Ammavan was a widower and had plenty of room for them. He welcomed them warmly and became Cherian’s father right away, since Cherian didn’t really know of any other and, in a short while, Lizzie, too, thought of him as her parent.

Her mother began to work as a typist-stenographer at the Travancore Legislative Assembly. It was a prestigious job, and Ammavan had remarked that his sister had begun to look less lonely. For some time everything had been fine, till her mother met Govinda Warrier—a powerful member of the Legislative Assembly, but married, Mrs. Nayar had confided to Lizzie, later.

Soon after meeting Govinda Warrier, her mother and Jose Ammavan had begun to argue incessantly. Lizzie remembered those days with dread, for her mother looked sad, angry and happy all at once. She often fell into violent fits of sobbing and took pains to dress carefully and looked ethereally beautiful.

She hardly had any time for Cherian. Barely nine, Lizzie shouldered the responsibility of taking care of Cherian. Lizzie didn't mind that at all. She loved her brother. But Ammavan got irritated at seeing Lizzie carrying Cherian all the time. Then her mother began to come late from work and Lizzie had to do the cooking in addition to the other chores.

Sometimes her mother would go to Cherian with her arms outstretched. "Come here my baby," she'd coo, but Cherian would cling to Lizzie and her mother would get upset with Lizzie and Jose Ammavan would get upset with her mother. It was terrible.

When her mother's body had been found at the upper balcony of the Assembly building, late one night, Lizzie began to understand what it meant when something didn't quite fit, like a body too large for its blouse. Jose Ammavan blamed Warrier; others claimed she had taken her own life; and the police said that she had slipped and fallen. Lizzie only remembered her mother as being sure-footed.

Lalitha Amma, her mother's boss, wrote a poem titled, "Beauty Lives Forever" that she recited at her mother's burial. It was a 10-line poem, and Lizzie had tried to memorize the words. But that first day, she forgot two lines, the third day, she forgot the middle paragraph and by the end of two weeks she couldn't remember anything other than the title.

Jose Ammavan kept Lizzie home for two weeks after her mother's death, but when she finally went back to school, the words "that's her," or "that's her daughter," began to follow her around. The pronoun often accompanied a quick facial tilt. Lizzie's existence became marked and labeled by a possessive pronoun. Her.

When she asked Jose Ammavan, why he thought Govinda Warrier would have killed her mother, he'd said that she was too young to understand but sometimes people become inconveniences.

"Even someone as beautiful as Amma?" she'd probed and Jose Ammavan had remarked that in life wealth was the most powerful aphrodisiac and beauty only skin-deep."

Traitorous, treacherous, short-lived love, Mrs. Nayar had explained, the length of a breath.

Lizzie remembered meeting Govinda Warrier, once. It had been many years ago, a few months after her mother's passing. Lizzie and Ammavan had gone to the fish market to buy some *chemmeen* and she'd noticed a middle-aged man, short, with a large nose and small, deep eyes that had appeared like sinking ships in the ocean of his large face. He'd been with his wife and two children, both older than Lizzie, one a boy who'd seen her staring and had stared right back making monkey faces at her, and a daughter about a year younger with a fastidiously neat look about her. The girl had stood with her father as he haggled down the price of *chemmeen*, her hair confined to two tight braids. She wore white shoes on her feet and a pretty floral dress that flowed around her ankles, just short of the ground.

She was most likely not the sort to play hopscotch or use the skipping rope, Lizzie had thought. The mother had long dark hair that hung almost to her hips, and wore a rich red silk sari with a purple border and plenty of jewelry on her hands: bangles, bracelets and rings. Her plump lower lip looked like it had once strongly reacted to a caustic comment and had never managed to resume its original contour.

"Why do rich people need to haggle?" she'd asked Jose Ammavan, "It's not like they cannot afford the price!" Jose Ammavan had laughed and said that she was getting to be pretty smart before glancing at the man she had pointed to.

"Let's go," he'd said suddenly and urgently.

Lizzie had hurried after Jose Ammavan as he left the fish stall, much to the annoyance of the stall owner who'd rained abuse as they'd walked away.

They hadn't taken more than five steps when a voice called out, "Jose, wait." It was the rich, big-nosed man.

Jose Ammavan stopped in his tracks but hadn't turned. Lizzie had looked curiously from one man to the other.

"Wait, Jose," the man called out, running to catch up. "Is this her daughter?" he'd asked pointing with his chin at Lizzie. It was the pronoun again. Closer, he looked older than he had standing with his peacock wife. There was gray along his temples and pouches beneath his deep-set eyes.

"Leave us alone, Warrier. Haven't you done enough?" Ammavan said furiously before grabbing Lizzie's hand and marching away. Lizzie had turned back to look at the man and had seen threads of her mother lingering and clinging to the stranger. She had wanted to take her mother back from the man. He had his mouth slightly open, his white teeth visible, and his deep dark eyes empty. The man looked sad, but that sadness did not belong to him. It belonged to them.

Lizzie wondered if it would have been better to be motherless as an infant than inherit the sordidness of her mother's death. It was painful to look back and Lizzie very seldom did, but it was in these moments of luminous clarity that she was forced to consider what could have been. Lizzie had recently fallen into that chasm between youth and adulthood. Her nerves jangled acutely to pain and pleasure and the one sometimes blended into the other. It was five years since her mother's death and yet the taint of it never seemed to dull. Lizzie reflected that life with Jose Ammavan was built on the understructure of loss, her father's and then her mother's. She wondered if Jose Ammavan's affection was tinged with the kind of feeling that ill fortune bestows: caution and overwhelming pity?

But, this time Pity Thomas had gone too far, resurrecting all her pain with his hurtful gibe. "Let go of my hand, Chechi, you're hurting me," Cherian said trying to pull his hand free of Lizzie's grasp. Lizzie relaxed and let him go.

"What did Pity mean? Why did he say that word?" Cherian asked in a high-pitched tremulous voice.

"If ever I hear you use that word, I'll wash your mouth with salt and soap!" Lizzie responded angrily. Then looking at Cherian's crestfallen face, "I'm sorry, Cherian. Don't worry about it. I love you. Now remember that!" The syllables curled around her mouth, softening her lips and making her seem wise beyond her years.

She remembered a story Jose Ammavan had told her just before her mother had died. An aging widowed woman retired to a village, deep in the Southwestern Ghats, where the thick evergreen foliage sucked up the monsoon rains even before reaching the soil. The widow had forsaken town life after her husband and child had died of a fever that had swept their entire village, leaving just a handful of hardier people behind.

She had built a small hut there and resided in contemplation of her lost loves and her still beating heart. She cooked one simple meal a day and learned to deny the beasts of hunger that beset her periodically with the berries that surrounded her.

One morning she had opened the door to her hut to encounter a wolf dog lying at her doorstep, injured. She had offered the creature water, and nursed its injury. She named the wolf dog, Chennaya, and shared her food with him. He slept on her doorstep every night and thus he became hers.

Periodically she would come to town for a few supplies and would command her wolf dog to stay within the edge of the forest so that the fearful villagers wouldn't attack her animal.

Soon after Chennaya made his appearance in her life, she noticed a change in her physical appearance. Men started noticing her when she went to town, and her water reflection showed her a picture of a celestial beauty with smooth skin, enlarged eyes and no trace of gray in her hair. In town, she met a well-muscled man who told her how beautiful she was. He followed her everywhere she went, singing praises to her exquisite beauty. He came from a long line of warriors and lived in a privileged section of the town.

One day he followed her to the forest's edge and upon seeing the wolf dog, he prepared to take out his bow and arrow. He was surprised and needed some convincing that Chennaya was indeed her pet. "See, he's tame," she called out, as Chennaya licked the hand she held out. "Don't ever follow me, though. He's a fierce protector," she said as she walked away into the forest with her wolf dog at her heels.

She found herself going to town more frequently, besieged by thoughts of her handsome warrior. Each time, the man would follow her all the way back to the edge of the forest.

Then one day, unable to contain himself the warrior decided to find out where the woman and her animal lived. He followed their tracks all the way into the forest. Finally, he saw signs of a clearing up ahead.

Buoyed at the thought of meeting his love, he walked rapidly towards the hut. It was only the sound of a low growl that alerted him to the animal's presence. The man reached for his knife just as the animal pounced on him. The man dug his knife into Chennaya's throat as the wolf dog opened its jaws on his left arm. Chennaya fell back letting out a loud yelp. Hearing the noise, the widow woman came rushing out and ran to the injured wolf dog. Blood gurgled out of Chennaya's throat and his yellow eyes began to seep color. The wolf dog breathed its last as soon as the woman laid her hand on its head. The moment Chennaya died, some chemical composition in the woman's physical appearance altered and before the horror struck warrior's eyes, the woman's hair grayed, her eyes aged and her skin took on the pallor of loss. The man ran back to the town quick as can be, shuddering at the thought of the woman with her lined face and old eyes.

The story had scared Lizzie when she'd first heard it. Now she was reconciled to it. She felt as though the story had something to do with her mother. Just like the widow-woman, her mother's life had been a mere façade, lost to her even before her death.

Lizzie looked at Cherian and noticed that his cheeks were wet. She stopped and pulled her brother's warm body towards her. She hugged him tightly. The sky darkened and a flock of seagulls scaled the clouds heading towards the ocean.

Lizzie rocked her brother just as Jose Ammavan had done when he'd heard of her mother's death. But Ammavan had been crying then. If she was weeping, she did not know it.

Jose Ammavan was sitting at the small table doing accounts when Lizzie and Cherian walked in. "I need a new blouse," she said loudly, too loudly. "This one doesn't fit anymore."

The Little Matter of Fresh Meadows Feces

Dear Vishnu,

You and Sarala left a great big vacuum in Fresh Meadows Apartment with your absence. Unanticipated problems have arisen and we have a pressing need for your sage counsel.

Our slum neighbors across the greens are raising a stink. They have taken to utilizing the north wall of our apartment gutters as their private toilets, depositing their daily earnings every morning.

Due to the workers strike, the garbage truck has not arrived for a month, despite weekly assurances from the Sanitation Department of the Bangalore Mahanagar Palike. We should never have named the place Fresh Meadows Apartments to begin with.

Last night we held our monthly General Body meeting and I was elected the Association's Acting President till your return. On the agenda was the issue of raising apartment dues. The money was to be applied to the installation of an air freshening system, given our current stinking situation; repainting the boundary wall, to deter the depositors; and upgrading our broken treadmill in the gym. Mrs. Vimala objected to the last, indicating that she doesn't use the gym and those who do use it can contribute toward the upgrade. An unpleasant argument erupted between Mrs. Reeta and Mrs. Vimala. It turns out that Mrs. Reeta will not be contributing to the gardener's salary since she lives in an "upstairs" flat and has no real need for a gardener. Mrs. Vimala and Mrs. Reeta exchanged words; a few of them off color and finally Mrs. Vimala left the meeting calling us assembled members "jackasses" as she walked away. Unfortunately we had to agree to table the issue till the next meeting.

As for the garbage strike, like you had suggested in your last letter, I sent an email to the Councillor, Mr. Manjunath on April 21. What should we do next? The apartment manager has asked us to protest as a group. Please advise.

Yours respectfully and truly,

Mohan Seshan, B.A. Economics

****

Dear Sarala,

I made pongal today. I added something new to the

recipe. I ground up some steamed carrots, mint and cashew nuts and added it to the rice. My son declared that I was a temperamental cook and my husband claimed it didn't taste any different at all. Why do I bother?

Mohan mentioned that he'd written to Vishnu about our feces problem. It's becoming quite unbearable, you know. We moved into the apartment thinking that the slums were too far off across the field and wouldn't really impact us. The field was like a green ocean separating us from them. But lately the slums seem to be closing in. The early morning shitters have chosen to use the drains and gutters close to our boundary wall as their bathroom. Our bedroom windows cannot be opened. The morning stench is sickening. What do these people eat, anyway? And the flies have begun to feast on the shit. So we spent some extra money this month installing netting on all our doors and windows. It's funny how paranoid Mohan has become. He does not allow the netting to be opened for any reason. When the milkman comes, he's given a small sliver to squeeze through. Mohan calls it the infestation of the fecal feeding insects and it would be so funny if it were not happening to us.

Mohan suggested all we apartment residents band together and picket in front of the Bangalore Mahanagar Palike offices. But, I'm wary of these protests. Protesters are usually rabble-rousers and to think that we could become one of them is quite appalling.

Tell me about America, Sarala, and every wonderful thing that's happening to you,

Prema Seshan, Temperamental Chef

****

Entry in Mita's diary:

Some fucking crap is breaking here. Grampa and Gramma from India are staying with us and they've been talking crazy. Somethin' about the slummers shitting behind their building. Gramma read out some crazy woman's letter last night about the smell of turd hitting their tiny matchbox flat—at dinner that too. They've lost it, turned senile. What's with India anyway? Leave the slum dogs alone. If you don't want them to crap outside, call them in and offer your toilets, I say. The letter started with some new recipe for pongal. Mom makes that sometimes. Smells a block away and looks like shit.

House is filled with India.

Mom's tough to deal with even without these old folks

around. Now it's like she's a newb. Dad's cool. Sometimes, I look at him and it's like he knows what I'm thinking.

New one here, Gramps wants me to pray to the Hindus before going to school every day. So I knelt and recited the Hail Maryjuana nice and loud. Mom burst into tears. That idiot Hans repeated the words after me. Oh Buddha-Allah-Rama-Krishna-Christ if you had to give me a brother, could you not have come up with something halfway intelligent?

Gramma doesn't like me. I can see it in her black obsidian eyes. Cool that SAT word. Comes in useful sometimes. Staring, she's always staring without saying a word. Then when I talk, she stares some more. I thought they knew English. Then she looks at Mom and asks her what I'd said and Mom repeats what I said in English. Crazy that. So yesterday, I asked Gramma if she liked crime shows on TV. Used Mom's Indian accent to say it and I got grounded for that. Grounded! Can't do nothing right.

I made salad for dinner and Mom hissed do you have to do this? Can't you eat like the rest of us? I ask, can't you eat like the rest of us, mom? Her eyes shine obsidian-like, just like her mother's. Leave me alone, Mom, leave me alone. But Dad plucks the words from my mouth and says it out aloud. Leave her alone, Madhu. Let her eat what she wants. Then they argue. The grandparents get into it and I take my salad and head to my room. And that little shit Hans screams in his wobbly voice, she's taking food to her room. Traitor, that one, gobbling Mom's food like there's no tomorrow. He's fat, I told Mom and she said that it's normal to be this chubby at that age. Yes in Plumpland. I know the kid is made fun of. Why doesn't she get it?

****

Dear Reeta,

What was all that about you and Vimala? Though, I have to admit she can test anyone's patience. Remember the time, she picked up two Dobermans from the vet and taught the dogs to pee in the toilet but forgot to mention that her pet parakeet was not part of their lunch? She'd purchased the bird for twice what it cost her for the two dogs together. And then there was that other time she chased her maid down the street for wearing provocative clothes, claiming the poor girl was enticing her husband into wrongdoing.

Tolerance was ever your strength, my dear Reeta. What made you so upset? Make peace, my dear. I know, I know, it is hard to deal with a woman like Vimala. We have managed to ignore her tantrums in the past. Chalk this down as another mental strength training exercise. I wish I were there to help.

Vishnu and I are settling into Madhu's life here. My granddaughter, Mita, is almost seventeen and Hans is fourteen, both teenagers now. Vishnu and I have trouble understanding them when they speak. Mita is given to a diet more suited to horses: oats, carrots, apples, salads, nuts and raisins. Hans is a little overweight. He will thin down when he reaches his full height, I think. Madhu is very busy and I am proud of all that she has achieved, at work and at home. She has Vishnu's persevering trait and my enduring one.

The thing I miss the most, the most, is the sound of our doorbell. What a joyous sound that—pealing the arrival of a friend. There is curiosity and connection in that sound. It is the feeling of a gift being unwrapped.

Imagining the trill of your doorbell,

Sarala Chandran

****

Dear Respected and Esteemed Chief Minister of the State of Karnataka,

In the last elections, my wife and I voted for you because we believed you have what it takes to turn this state around, make it cleaner, greener and safer. But corruption has continued to bleed into our daily lives, the only green is on the ficus trees inside our homes and safety is a matter best taken up with the street lords. It is a basic citizen's right to expect civic cleanliness, at the least a timely removal of the mounds of garbage and the defecated remnants from dogs, cows, pigs and humans. When the Sanitation Department of the Bangalore Mahanagar Palike fails in that fulfillment, I have no choice but to bring the matter to your august attention.

Despite complaining to the Sanitation Department of the Bangalore Mahanagar Palike, on April 21, May 3, May 15, and May 21, I have received no response. The situation is unbearable and unhealthy and if you don't take this matter in hand, my next letter will be to the editor of the *Deccan Herald*.

I am a retired handicapped government employee, having worked for the Indian Railways for over four decades, fifteen of them after having lost the toes on my left foot due to an accident, the result of post-accident gangrene. I feel that I have sacrificed myself in service to this great nation.

I paid for and have the right to demand a clean environment. I expected to spend my remaining years, living on my pension, enjoying the quiet comfort of my home. Unfortunately, due to no fault of mine, both quiet and comfort are being compromised.

Please respond at your earliest.

Humbly,

Vishnu Chandran, resident of Flat 8B, Fresh Meadows Apartment, M.A, LLB

****

Dearest Prema,

Madhu made pongal yesterday exactly the way you'd described and we all enjoyed it, except Mita, who eats only salads for dinner. What discipline my grandchild has. You'll be amazed. She is so thin and delicate, but there's a small stone in her eyes and a granite block on her shoulders. I remember how we were at that age, so I feel sorry for the child. She was such a beautiful baby. And I feel sorry for Madhu. This life is very different from ours, Prema, and I cannot describe it other than to say that the quiet is ominous and the chatter is disturbing.

The I in this country is dominant. Ipad, Ipod, I peed, I paid, I went, I came, I, I, I. Vishnu chastised me yesterday for requesting that we go back home. He said that as a mother I should be used to sacrificing for my child. Well I am, but my child is all grown up and sacrificing for her own children. I can't help it if I'd rather deal with the feces problem in Fresh Meadows.

Vishnu and I often reminisce about India and I can see that Mita and Hans find our details boring. They don't relate to our India. That's as it should be, they've only known this country.

Initially they were fascinated and asked all the clichéd American questions. Are there elephants on the road? Yes, the overweight human kind. Have you seen any snakes? Yes, the ones who smile and tell you they'll help you cross the road and then you find your wallet missing. Why do men pee in public places? It's an animal instinct. Just like dogs piss on other dogs' piss, men piss when they see other men piss. Do people know English? No answer to that one.

In all the obvious ways my daughter lives a good life. They have a beautiful home filled with beautiful furniture and all the latest gadgets. They have two wonderful children. They are used to doing things for themselves without relying on servants and the like, and both Madhu and Suri have great jobs. But they rarely have time to enjoy what they have. Madhu is so preoccupied that she rarely has time to talk. Suri is seldom at home and even when he is, he is quiet most of the time.

I feel as though I'm living in someone else's skin here. There's a particular sadness to this perfect life.

Vishnu wrote a letter to the Chief Minister of Bangalore about our feces problem. Since he hadn't heard from them in a week, he wrote a letter to the *Deccan Herald*, but he hasn't heard back from the editor too. Something will come about. Have patience, dear Prema, and send us a new recipe in your next letter.

What's Vimala been doing lately? Has she reconciled with Reeta? It's rather tragic that the two of them are unable to get along. Prema, you must step in and help. Call the two of them over to your house for your delicious besan laddoo. I know no one can resist the pull of that melting sweetness. Then remind Reeta that we all feast our eyes on the flowers in the garden. Let's not be miserly about little nothings. We have a lot more to worry about than flowers and who works out in the Gym. Remind the two of them that we live in a community and our decisions should benefit all.

Persuade Vimala to allow for Reeta's feelings. Do you remember the old Vimala? She arrived at Fresh Meadows about eight years into her marriage.

I remember how she'd get all dressed up to go dancing on Friday nights. I remember she once wore a brocade, purple, sleeveless blouse with pink silk harem pants. Ahhh how we envied her, her style, her freedom and her exuberance. She'd step out of her flat leaving a trail of perfume behind. Once someone pinned a note near the staircase, "And Vimala was here!" Do you remember that? We never did find out who it was.

It's about different lifestyles. While she went out to parties and dinners, you stayed home caring for your kids, cleaning, cooking, making house. It's more than likely that she envied you and Reeta and the others while you all envied her. She had the freedom to travel and work long hours. And you didn't. I must add that recently I've begun to notice a change in her—a slower descent down the stairs, and an emptiness in her eyes.

I doubt she sets out to be insensitive. She needs to care. She needs to know that she cares. I remember she came over once, when she had just moved in to the apartment, with some chicken soup when she heard Vishnu was sick. I didn't tell her that Vishnu was vegetarian.

Vimala tried to be a part of our evening gatherings in the garden while the kids played. But our talk was all about our children. I know I've mentioned this before but I do wonder why she never adopted. A child would have helped ground her. Now she just seems to be floating, looking for ways to connect. Maybe her little rebellion at the General Body meeting was her way to make her presence felt.

We await letters from all of you with as

much desperation as you await the Sanitation Department's truck.

Longing for Indian shores,

Sarala Chandran

****

Entry in Mita's diary

Can't get over it. Some days it hurts somethin' crazy. It's the two lives I lead. One the fuckin fake one at home. Mom goes on about grades. Little does she know that I'm the brown bird that is curly fried. I don't give a fucking crap about grades. Yesterday, I had a dream about my body being used as a tennis ball, lobbed from side to side. I felt the pain of each *thwack* against me, and then I was flung over the net, spinning like a ball, before receiving another *thwack*. And it went on endlessly. I couldn't make out the players. Maybe it was Tom both sides. Fucking Tom. Running from one end of the court to the other. Teaching me calculus and then telling me to meet him in his office to discuss my college recs and promising me Pete's iced mocha if I showed up. Only there was no ice and no mocha in his office late in the evening, when only the jocks were huddled in the gym. There was only Pete. Afterwards he told me he'd write my recommendations that same evening.

Asked Tamara later if she'd believe it if Tom Camden would ever do what he did. And she said, Don't Be Fucking Ridiculous, with that unbelievable brow shake.

****

Dear Vishnu,

This is a short note to inform you that a reporter from the *Deccan Herald* came by yesterday and asked for you. I told him that you were out of town. He came prepared with a surgical mask to cover his nose and mouth and then began to interview me and a few other residents including Prema and Mrs. Reeta. I asked him if he understood how we felt and if it was feasible for us to walk around the whole day, in the sweltering heat, with a mask on our faces. He seemed to understand. He has taken some pictures of the dried feces lying near the wall. We will hopefully see something in the newspaper in the next few days.

We had our monthly Association meeting again. We discussed the *Deccan Herald* reporter at first.

We decided to hold the treadmill upgrade till you come back, even though we could have arrived at a resolution, without the presence of Mrs. Vimala.

In humble acknowledgment,

Mohan Seshan, B.A. Economics

****

Dear Mohan,

I am inordinately pleased to inform you that I did finally hear from the editor of *The Deccan Herald*. They are publishing my letter along with some pictures, which the reporter took when he came to Fresh Meadows Apartment. It is scheduled to appear in the June 18th issue. Once the article is published, the Sanitation authorities will talk to and convince the slum dwellers to stop shitting by or near our building. Make sure you keep a cutting of the article and pictures and send them to me, if you can.

All is otherwise fine here in California.

Vishnu Chandran, Scribe

****

Dear Prema,

The longer I stay here, the less I understand happiness. I went for a walk to the park with Vishnu yesterday. At the park, three boys approached us soon after we sat down on a bench. They started chatting with Vishnu, asking him where he was from and what I was wearing. They seemed to be Mexican though Vishnu and I can never make out the difference between people here. Suddenly one of them took out a knife and started playing with it. Just tossing it from one palm to another like a tennis ball.

One of the boys then said, in an ominous tone, "Got some cash, old man?" but he was looking at me. You cannot fathom how scared I was. We were being mugged in broad daylight. I was terrified Vishnu would do something stupid. So I pretended to have not heard what they said and began to speak.

I spoke of the feces on the north wall of our apartment building and described how Vimala refused to agree to upgrade the gym equipment, and your recipe for pongal; about the fecal feeding insects and how we hung our clothes to dry in the backyard one day and Vishnu's undershirt flew into the neighbor's yard and how angry Mita was when she heard this; and how Suri is so quiet and how Madhu works all the time and how our granddaughter eats green leaf, nuts, oats and apples—horse food mostly, and so many things I don't know how I carried on or why. All I knew was that if I stopped they would kill us, so I didn't dare stop speaking. Vishnu looked as though he would interrupt at first but then he stayed silent while I went on and on. All of a sudden one of the boys started laughing. He called us crazy kooks. Then they got up and left. Simply left. Vishnu and I made our way back home feeling ten years older than we were.

In the evening we told Madhu and Suri what had happened. They wanted to call the police. We convinced them that was not the right thing to do, it would just lead to unnecessary complications. Nothing had really happened. Now at least, Vishnu is convinced that we are putting a burden on Madhu and Suri and has begun to talk of going back home,

Scared and unhappy,

Sarala Chandran

****

Dear Madhu, my daughter,

I have noticed your anxiety. I am unwilling to impose on it. I write this letter, even while I live in your house. The distance between us has become wide. We talk but it's perfunctory. I wish we can be forthright with each other. Looking back, it is clear that we have discoursed most honestly through our letters to each other. Remember how it was when you were growing up? When you were in college, our discussions ranged into so many diverse areas. We differed on many: communism, Mrs. Gandhi, euthanasia. Yet we held strongly to our opinions. I've always believed that opinion is the guts of reason. Have you ever felt the want of our exchanges lately?

I have noticed that you and Mita are constantly arguing. It is not like the arguments we used to have. Teenagers are volatile. You were the same. But I see in your daughter what I have never encountered in you. This is not a criticism of Mita. Just an observation. Don't rush to defend your daughter, my daughter, since you know I am deeply concerned.

Dear daughter, I saw you sitting in your car in the driveway yesterday. I was standing at the living room window and watching you. I don't know what you were sitting there for, but I can guess the reasons.

I must confess that we also know about Suri. He left lying on the kitchen table a letter from his Human Resources Department giving him notice from his job. I'm sorry I read the letter, but it was lying there forgotten and I assumed it was junk mail like all the other letters that lie on the table.

I wish I could help. It is easier to deal with the world's problems than the ones in our own homes. The only thing your mother and I can think of doing is to relieve you of the burden of keeping up a front. Again, this is not a criticism, don't take it as one. We have decided to go back to India. It's not about the incident in the park or Suri losing his job or anything else that is going on here. It's about our connection. It is strongest when we are apart.

I hope you will forgive me.

Always, Dad

****

Dear Sarala,

You sound wistful and sad. That is unlike you. You were looking forward to this trip to your daughter's house with so much anticipation.

Even though Vimala does push my buttons, I must remind you about something she said on the day that her pet parakeet died, when we trooped into her house to express sympathy. About being able to roll with the punches. She was right. But, it is harder to deal with life's punches when we age. Heck when did we become old? Ok, Sorry, no more platitudes, I promise.

Here, we celebrated with some chocolate cake and Sula wine the day the Sanitation truck arrived to take our garbage away. Finally the strike is over and yesterday's garbage is gone. I won't worry about tomorrow's trash.

Love,

Reeta, Lover of chocolate, wine and roses

****

Entry in Mita's Diary

Apparently Gramps' letter got published in the newsies. And the slummers have been asked to take their shit elsewhere or else and the brown nosers painted over the shit stains. Whatever. I'm going to puke if I hear them say the f word one more time. Fucking feces.

I was walking to my room today and I saw Gramps take off his shoes and socks and show Hans his toeless foot. That was fucking eerie. Like a headless corpse.

That's the old man's redemption. I posted on Facebook and hit 89 likes in like 30 motherfucking minutes. How's that for interest? Hans copied my post and I took down his Facebook. The whiny weasel complained to Mom. Now it's my fault again.

Had enough. It's Hans this and Hans that. If that overweight turd robbed the place, Mom, Gramma and Gramps would say, *beta*, it's ok. Don't do it again, ok? Every fucking word is a head nod. What's to love?

The neighbor came over yesterday to complain that Gramps' garment flew into their backyard. What the fuck garment? Turned out it was an undershirt. Scared the neighbor kid would rat me out in school on top of everything else. But, he didn't say anything. I glared at Mom when the neighbor left and she asked me what? As though it was my fault.

Last week Mom caught me doing happy grass. Well she didn't really catch me. She found my stash hidden in my boots. Why the fuck she'd want to clean my boots? Her face was as green as the weed she held and grabbed me and made me watch while she flushed the stuff down the toilet. Dad, poor dad, ain't his fault, but you wouldn't know that by the way Mom carried on.

All this culture is de-pressing. Here they are, the oldies, carrying on about some shit in a different country in the different language they fucking call English when our world here is a shit mess. Let's hear Gramps write about that. I heard Mom tell Gramma that I would come around and that I was Indian at heart. After all Indian is half of Indian American. Gramma nodded her head and said she understood. Understood what?

If only Mom understood. Stuffing the kid and making him fucking weak. Have a feeling he rage-eats. The moron can't even defend himself in the shit closet. Does she even know? Tried to show Hans some self-def moves, but the boy's slow. Told him to hit the treadmill. Told Mom to cut down his intake and she stared at me as though I'd lost it. Told me I'm putting the brat down by calling him fat. Mom lives her own fucking version.

The oldies are getting ready to leave. At night, Gramma came to me and said she'd saved up some money and handed me a wad. Spend it wisely beti, she said. Woke up this morning thinking of the weed.

The Smell of Jasmine

She sniffs a couple of times, hoping the lingering smell of jasmine would go away. Is there a stray jasmine plant outside the bedroom window? She gets up from bed and peers outside. It's dark, the kind of darkness that is metallic and grim. Nona can't quite make out the plants she knows are there: her prize pink and yellow roses, the sweet-williams, foxgloves and her annuals: snapdragons, petunias and marigolds. In the morning, she tells herself, she will inspect each and every shoot and sapling and instruct the gardener to uproot everything and make the soil virgin again. She'd inherited the gardener along with the house. What was the man's name now, Raju or Ramu? Drat! It was impossible to keep these servants' names straight. A breeze blows the curtains towards her. The white jacquard silk covers her face and the jasmine smell disappears, replaced by fingers of sweat and spice. It's malodorous and malevolent. She frees herself from the curtains, violently clawing her way out.

She goes back to the bed. The rhythmic clicking of the fan drowns out Anjan's snores. She lies on the bed and curves her body towards Anjan. The cloying jasmine smell spreads around her again. She feels it enter her body and take up residence inside her veins; pumping odor with blood, infusing the organs in her body: her small intestine, her heart and her throat. It presses down on her. She holds her breath and clutches her left forearm tightly. Squeezes herself, and feels the blood push to the outside of her grasp. She holds on, despite the pain, willing the smell away. She can almost feel the radius and the ulna.

In the morning, she examines the large bruise near her elbow. It looks like a jasmine flower. It has four slender petals and one thick stem.

Later, at Somalee's house, she stretches out her left arm as she hands over a James Patterson novel. Her three quarter length wide sleeves fall away and Somalee's eyes are drawn to the bruise and she utters in a stricken, choked voice, "What is that, Nona?" Nona lets her sleeves fall back and puts her arm behind her back, whispering hurriedly, "Nothing, nothing, Som."

She waits for the phone call, which comes almost an entire day later, "Does he hurt you, Non?" She arranges the words of her answer carefully, "No, Som, not generally." The word, *generally*, stretches like an elastic band to snap shut on Somalee's suspicions. Then Somalee proceeds to talk about a social worker, Tina, who is absolutely the best at her work, besides being discreet. Poor Anjan, she thinks, smiling to herself, complacent in his well-tended life, unaware of the rising rumors of his misuse.

Nona remembers the time she'd first met Anjan. She'd known right away he was her man. He'd been slight and bespectacled, with an air of distraction, an absent mindedness that drew her. She'd pursued and wooed him into acknowledging her and then a month later he'd bought her some jasmine flowers, bagged together. The cheapest and most commonly available flower: jasmine, her mother had remarked. She'd put her face into the bag and inhaled. She'd asked him to marry her while her face had still been inside the bag. Her eyes had peered up at him and her breath had blown the bag out like a balloon. He'd looked at her brown-bagged face and said, "I need to check with my parents." Like it was a course sign-up for college. She'd nodded, thinking that in time, that statement would be, "I need to check with my wife."

Dressing for her wedding, she'd chosen a tiara of jasmine, because it had complimented her skin tones and the angular bones of her face. Her mother had seen her with the flowers on her hair and told her peremptorily to take it off. "You look cheap," she'd shouted, "only servant girls and prostitutes wear jasmine." Nona had hurriedly taken it off and sprayed herself with Dior's Hypnotic Poison.

They moved to the United States after the wedding. They'd been married now for nine years. When the U.S. had declared war against Iraq, Anjan had begun to look back at India longingly. Watching Anjan railing at Bush's policies at every dinner party had been tedious and predictable. Isn't that why she'd married him though, for his predictability? His remarks represented a journey that followed the same route, day after day, with no chance of derailment. She herself followed Indian news avidly and didn't care to discuss U.S. policies.

Nona and Anjan had done well in the U.S., starting off in a small apartment in Sunnyvale and then buying a house atop a small mountain in Saratoga with views of the valley. Anjan co-founded his first venture within a few months of their Sunnyvale apartment life. She remembered the birth of his company. She'd worn her gold lamé dress with black stilettos. She'd gone to the salon and had her hair swept up in a do. The stylists at the Piccadilly Salon had gathered around her admiring her beauty. Over champagne at The Plumed Horse, they'd thrown out names for the company. Anjan had insisted on Anon Solutions. She'd been flattered.

It is now almost a month since they'd moved back to India. The first few days had been exhilarating. Nona quickly adjusts to her new expatriate status. The moment she sets her Jimmy Choo'd feet on India's shore, she becomes the person she knows she is.

Dining at the Khyber Pass restaurant, her head lifts and her eyes sweep across to the waiter who'd served her water without ice. He comes running to assist her with a slavish air. She is well versed in this language of mistress and slave. This is the first time in nine years she feels in total control.

But India inexplicably has changed Anjan, too. It is the same Anjan, but now back in India, among others like him, he looks at her differently, contradicts her, talks over her, and complains about tiredness when she initiates sex. She reasons that his business problems are probably weighing him down. He is stressed from shouldering the full responsibility of establishing a corporate identity in India. He has to deal with all the hiring and wrangling with lawyers and agents who claim to help smooth the way. Every time she questions him, he says "everything's ok," which is a lie, for she knows that the building he'd planned to rent slipped out of his grasp. He is still looking for something just right. If only he were a bit more assertive, her mother remarks, these problems wouldn't occur. She responds to her mother's criticism with, "I love him, Ma."

Nona practices her hidden language on servants, workmen, waiters and shop girls.

"I asked for tea and biscuits about fifteen minutes ago," she addresses the temporary cook, Kamlesh, "Did you figure it would make me fat?" Nona stretches in her leotards displaying her athletic physique to full advantage.

Nona and Anjan move into their rented bungalow in Noida. She redecorates the place in a record fourteen days with the help of a crew of three men commissioned to assist her from Anjan's office. Everything has to be perfect. She supervises them, pointing with her index finger and shaping her whole hand like a gun while giving rapid-fire orders and counter orders. She can see the frustration on the men's faces, but they are powerless and Nona exults in her own nuclear force. The Christian boy Jimmy Pereira thinks he can get the better of her and sits down on the couch exclaiming, "Let me know when you're sure you want that art piece on that wall." She smiles at him sweetly and then bends to pick up a small string from the floor. Her wide necked peasant blouse gapes and she sees Jimmy looking straight down her neckline. She is glad she is wearing her red Victoria's Secret push ups. When she stands up, she meets Jimmy's eyes, and sees that he understands her hunger.

At the end of two weeks, her house is almost ready for the first party, exquisitely furnished and arted up. There are beautiful gallery pieces on every wall. Nona walks through the house and memorizes the names of each artist and practices and rehearses the walk-through speech. "This is an Anjolie Ela Menon, and this one a rather smallish one of Satish Gujral, I have one more of Gujral in the dining room, an impressive piece, Oh and this is Jamini Roy. I refuse to have any Husseins, so common, you know. Oh, Did I hear you say Amrita Sher-Gil? You didn't? I love women artists, don't you? Art is such a male dominated field. And here's my Sher-Gil. Wonderful, isn't it? You should get one. They're rather difficult to acquire. I'm lucky Mummy has connections. If I'd left it to poor Anjan, I'd have ended up with village scenes on every wall. And here's my pièce de résistance, a Cecil Burns. Can you believe this? Yes, it's an original! What else would I get? Fakes? You haven't heard of him? Hahaha, that's funny."

Nona speaks to her mother every morning after she finishes her workout. It is part of her routine now. This morning they talk about hiring servants. Her mother cautions her: "Whatever you do, do not let them sit on the couch or chair. Their place is on the floor. Put together an inventory of spoons, forks, knives and plates. Never mind the forks. They never steal forks."

Funny how she'd not gotten along with her mother when she'd been a teenager looking for a quick out from her I-told-you-sos. But now it is as though her mother is her best friend, an extension of herself. Her morning phone calls to her mother have become her anchor.

She inventories her cutlery and pastes the list to the inside of a kitchen drawer.

****

Nona is scheduled to interview three servants, two women and one man. The first woman is due to arrive any moment. It is early afternoon and as she sits on the couch, the sun reflects off her solitaire and flashes its brilliance on the ceiling. She moves her left hand and watches as the reflected shape blurs and oblates. The television is on and the news is of some corruption scandal. She watches the report, alliterating disaster headlines in her head: Slaughter in Sudan, Rampage in Rawalpindi, Tumult in Tehran, Mayhem in Mogadishu, Riots in Romania, Bomb blasts in Bombay, Jailed in Jakarta, Crackdown in China, Narcotics in New York, Protests in Paris, Violence in Venezuela. This is her creative exercise of the day.

When she opens the door to Sheela, the maid, she can only focus on the jasmine flowers tightly tucked into Sheela's braid. Before even letting her into the house, Nona dismisses her without giving her any reason. She can hear Sheela complain loudly about how she had to take two buses to get to Madam's house.

Within a few minutes her second candidate shows up. She sits on one of the chairs at the dining table, the base of which is a tree trunk with branches clawing out into supports. She rests one elbow on the table, her upper body a little hunched, and bids the man stand before her. Strangely and wonderfully enough, the man looks like Anjan. Thin and slight of frame, his eyes plead desperately.

"Your name?" she asks in Hindi.

"Raju, madam" he replies in Hindi with a strong Bihari brogue.

"What cooking experience do you have?"

"I worked at Gandhi Tea stall in Dariyaganj. I bought the shop along with my friend Ramu from my village. I made tea and samosas and poori-alu and dal and sabzi. Everyday. We had lots of customers. We were doing well."

"Why did you leave?"

"Madam, those *goondas*, MP Surya's men, they wanted *rupaiya* from me. I was already heavily in debt. I borrowed money to start the teashop. Most of my money went to pay the debt. I didn't want to pay the thugs. But they came in one night and broke all our tea glasses. We had to come up with more money to replace the glasses." He shrugged his shoulders and shook his head sadly; "Finally, I sold my share to Ramu."

"Ok. I'm willing to give you a chance. But I need someone who can stay in the house with us."

Raju nods his head vigorously, his voice rising excitedly. "I can stay, Madam. I can stay," he repeats. "My wife, Jamuna and I, we're newly wed. We got married just two months ago. She can clean your house and we can both sleep in the kitchen."

This was interesting, two for the price of one.

"Hmm, how old is Jamuna?"

"She's sixteen, madam. Very clever. She studied up to sixth grade, English medium school," he says with shining pride, holding up six fingers to indicate the level of Jamuna's English speaking abilities.

Nona thinks about having an English-speaking servant. She could invite Somalee and her American husband, John Turow and instruct the maid in English to make some hot tea. John and Som would be taken aback.

"Send Jamuna to me. I'll talk to her. Tomorrow in the afternoon."

With a nod Raju folds his hands together and leaves.

She doesn't bother opening her door to the third

candidate.

She calls her mother that afternoon immediately after Raju's departure.

"Dahling, what if the girl gets pregnant?" her mother asks her. "Have you thought of that? It's all well and good to get a married couple. They're going to have sex all the time. These people always do. They're not like us. And make sure they don't sleep in your kitchen. The smell of semen in the morning mixed with your oatmeal won't be very palatable."

The next afternoon, Raju reappears at the appointed time with a shy slight woman-child, a dark skinned creature with huge eyes that stare bemusedly at the paintings on the wall. The girl is dressed in a bright yellow nylon sari with shiny blouse sleeves encasing her thin arms.

"I'm going to speak in English. Raju said you attended an English school till sixth grade."

Jamuna nods her head, averting her face shyly.

"When did you get married?"

Her face is still averted and she doesn't reply.

"Talk to Madam, Jamuna," instructs Raju sternly in Hindi. But his eyes are anything but stern.

"Two months ago," Jamuna whispers back in Hindi.

"In English, Jamuna," Nona commands.

"Two mmm two mahnths."

"Can you make tea?"

"Yes," she nods her head vigorously.

"Have you worked in a house before?"

"No," Jamuna responds.

Good, at least the girl knows yes and no. She's certainly not needed to make conversation. Yes and no are more than adequate for serving as a maid, Nona muses. Nona is struck by how young and together the couple look. Jamuna's eyes are large and heavily lashed and Raju has a baby face that will probably give him a youthful look even when he's in his forties. Jamuna, on the other hand, is the quintessential Indian woman. Beautiful in her teens, jaded in her twenties, resilient in her thirties, tired in her forties and desperate in her fifties. By the second pregnancy, her thin arms and taut stomach will most likely sag and waffle.

"I hope you're not planning to have babies right away?"

Jamuna looks puzzled.

Nona repeats the question in Hindi and she can see Jamuna's cheeks heat up.

Raju looks down at his wife's head and nods. "Madam, God willing."

Nona shakes her head.

"Not good, Raju. I've been married for nine years and Sahib and I, we don't have children. We don't want children."

"Maaaad-am" exclaims Raju, looking shocked.

"How old are you, Jamuna?"

"Sixteen," she answers in Hindi, raising her head and her eyes focus on Nona. There's no trace of her earlier shyness. She would be the one to watch out for, thinks Nona.

"I like both of you," Nona says. Raju beams and starts to say something but Nona holds out her hand. "I like both of you," she repeats. "Come back tomorrow and I'll give you my answer."

That evening Nona calls her mother and launches her search for a cheap urologist.

The next day, Raju and Jamuna arrive just after Anjan leaves for work.

"I want both of you to live here. Your food will be free. Raju you'll cook and Jamuna you'll help him and take care of the house. I'm going to give you a bed, free meals and five thousand rupees every month. That's generous, right? But I need both of you to think about what I'm going to say. Let me tell you a secret. The reason why Anjan Sahib and I are rich is because we don't have children. I want you to think about that, ok?"

Jamuna responds in English, "We come and work, that all, please, thank you?"

There is a question in there somewhere thinks Nona. "Good English, Jamuna," she says in Hindi and smiles.

"Please, thank you," responds Jamuna in English, "But what you want us do, madam?"

Aha, the chit didn't want her husband to know what they were saying. Well, two can play that game. Nona put on her most refined accent and somehow despite the nine years in America, the words came out sounding British. "Either you or Raju can take care of it. It's easier if Raju does. It's not permanent. Later in a few years you can rethink the decision and reverse the operation, if that's what you wanted. To have babies, you understand, right? You're young. Right now, you should work and repay all your debts. I'll have a doctor here and Raju's operation can be performed right here. I'll pay all the bills and take care of you. As a bonus, I'm going to give you an extra twenty thousand rupees for the operation! You and he can both enjoy your money and become rich."

"I not unnerstand."

"Leave it to me, Jamuna," Nona assures her. "I'll take care of you and Raju. A doctor will come and make sure you won't accidently have a child. It'll take just a few minutes. The doctor will remove something from his *pishab* area. I'll pay for the operation and give you twenty thousand and both of you can live and work here and repay all your debts. A few years later, when you're old enough, the doctor can put what he removed back and you can have babies again. Amazing, right? Doctors these days can perform miracles!"

"Madam, what are you saying to Jamuna?" Raju asks fearfully in Hindi, sensing the unease in Jamuna's expression.

"Ask Jamuna, Raju, she understands. She's a smart girl. You should be really proud of her."

Raju beams and casts a proprietary look at his wife. Jamuna doesn't smile back.

"You've got a lot to think about, don't you? Sleep on it tonight and let me know tomorrow. Then next week you can start work here. Your future is all set. All your debts will be gone." Nona waves her elegant hands and the refraction of the diamond centers on Jamuna's eyes, filling her pupils with sudden brilliance.

The telephone rings later that evening, "I'm Tina

Saigal. Is this Nona Mehta?"

"Yes."

"Madam, are you doing ok?"

"Huh?"

"I'd like to come by and talk to you regarding options."

"What are you talking about? This is a wrong number."

"No, stop, don't hang up. I'm the social worker. Is he there? Is that why you don't want to talk?"

Everything clicks. She almost bursts out laughing. She pauses, collecting herself and responds quietly, "Yes."

"I want to help. I want to give you some options. We have lots of resources. Tell me when I can meet you."

Two days later, Raju and Jamuna move into the house. Jamuna is quiet and restrained and respectful. Nona really has nothing to criticize her about. Yet, Nona feels intimidated by the measure of Jamuna's eyes.

Nona sets the wheels in motion and with the help of her mother identifies Dr. Brahma, educated in Patna Medical College, who is willing to perform the sterilization. Indira Gandhi had it right, Nona thinks. India could be a much stronger country if these people were not birthing like mice. On the appointed day, the Doctor arrives and examines a terrified Raju. The doctor explains the procedure to Raju and Jamuna, in a mixture of Hindi, English and one French word. "I'll make a tiny slit on each side of your scrotum and pull out a piece of the vas deferens and then clamp it shut. voilà! All done. Simple!" The doctor's unctuousness disgusts Nona. But then she figures that the man doesn't really have anything to do with her. After the doctor's explanation, Jamuna runs outside. Nona sees the servant girl vomit into her petunias. Later, Nona tells herself, later she'll make Jamuna wash out every last leaf.

Raju and Dr. Brahma disappear into the guest room.

Jamuna stands outside the door facing it, as though wondering whether she should go in or not.

About forty minutes later, the doorbell rings and Nona yells out to Jamuna to find out who it is and to tell them to come later. Jamuna hadn't moved from outside the guestroom door all the while. She looks at Nona and almost reluctantly shuffles her way towards the door. Jamuna opens the door and Nona can hear her say that they are busy. A loud voice is heard retorting, "I'm not leaving until I meet her."

"Yes, may I help you?" Nona asks approaching the front door. A heavyset woman is standing outside arms akimbo.

"Nona? I'm Tina Saigal. The social worker. Let's find a quiet place to talk." She steps into the house, pushing Jamuna aside.

"I'm sorry, this is not a good time," Nona tells Tina.

"It never is, my dear. You've been putting me off. I want to help," she whispers earnestly. Nona can see that Jamuna is listening to the conversation. "I've come to take care of you. I've brought some medicines, salves and ointments." Tina points to her heavy green leather shoulder bag. In cases like these, women like you never go to the hospital. I am here to help. Show me your bruise."

Nona remembers her jasmine bruise. It's all but disappeared. "This is not a good time, Tina. I'm a little busy at the moment."

Just then the doctor emerges and rubs his hands together. "All done," he exclaims. The chap is resting. He can get up in an hour. Jamuna goes running into the guest room as soon as the doctor comes out. The sounds of her sobbing can be heard, loud and clear.

"What's going on, here?" Tina Saigal demands.

"Tina, I think you should leave. I cannot talk about

myself, or even think about myself at a time like this." Nona holds up a frail hand to her forehead. "I'm under a great deal of stress. I'll call you, I promise. First thing tomorrow."

The doctor takes out his card and hands it to Tina. "I'm Dr. Brahma," he introduces himself to Tina. The quack.

She lets them both out and the moment she does that Nona realizes she's made a mistake. She runs to the kitchen window that faces the street and watches as both of them stand by Doctor Brahma's car talking to each other. Isn't there patient confidentiality, she wonders?

The smell of jasmine enters the kitchen first. She turns and looks at Jamuna. Her eyes are severe and winter seems to have lined every muscle and fold on her face. Nona turns away reflecting on how common overwrought emotions can be.

Nona leaves the kitchen and as she walks away she can hear Anjan's car pulling into the driveway. She rushes to the door to greet him. Anjan looks embarrassed and irritated when she embraces him. He disengages and goes into the bedroom. Nona follows.

"What was that?" she questions Anjan.

Anjan looks grave, determined, "I'm sorry, I have

something to say," and his voice is cold and final.

Later, she goes back to the kitchen and begins to open all the drawers. Her cutlery drawer swings off its rails and the contents fly all over the kitchen floor. At the sound, Jamuna appears and stands at the doorway. "What do you want?" Nona yells, "What the fuck do you want?"

Jumble

The narrow, dark passageway inside the Diablo Apartment complex ground floor smells of the countries left behind. Fried fish, curry and cabbage. There's probably no getting away. I can hear the sound of the laundry. I have never walked down the hallway without hearing the sound of the dryer, no matter the time of day or night. I hold Quaid's hand as I climb up the stairs. The first floor landing is stained with spit, dirt and turmeric. We pull to a stop before 2A. Quaid pulls me into an embrace and gives me a quick kiss. With his breath still caught in mine, I use my key and open the door, step inside and shut the door behind me, leaving Quaid on the outside.

Nothing's changed inside. It is a familiar that I'm used to. But I attend to it this time. The room I have entered has been segmented into many. The dining area situated near the window has a table covered with a plastic cloth and in the middle, a vase with dusty plastic roses that were once red, and now have faded, exposing its pretense. The vase with the flowers has been there on that table since I can remember.

The walls in the dining area have a picture of my dead grandparents, side by side, with a thin garland of fake marigolds strung across the frames. Both, Daddyji and Mummyji look stiff and unreal.

To one side of the room, I see the reading area, two chairs with cushions and a footstool. The morning's *San Jose Mercury News* is on the footstool, folded down to the Lifestyle section. There is a cupboard against the wall and through the glass half of the cupboard, the bottles and glasses are visible, arranged neatly in rows.

Against the far wall, there is a television. My brother, my aunt and my father are sitting on a striped couch facing the set. The blue from the screen striates across their faces, like a lighthouse beacon.

"I've brought someone," I announce over the television volume.

The statement bounces and registers on each face in the room before hitting the television, where it is swallowed. Lily Mausi hits the mute button.

Manil cracks his knuckles and the sound is loud in the muted room. He begins to rock and Lily Mausi holds her fist out and upturned, attempting to calm Manil. But it doesn't help.

Manil rocks on the couch side to side.

"I've brought a friend. He's waiting outside."

"Who, Mira?" he asks. I soften my voice out of habit. "A friend, you'll like him."

Dad has his head turned towards me. On the table in front of him is a Chivas Regal bottle. He is wearing his holey, once white, undershirt. His graying chest hairs are poking ferociously through. There is a shirt hanging on one of the dining room chairs. I pluck it off the chair and hand it to him. Dad lifts and drops his shoulders as he gets into the shirt. But the movements also indicate perplexity.

I can sense my aunt looking worriedly at me as I open the door and pull Quaid in.

"This is Quaid," I introduce. "Quaid, this is Manil, my brother. That's my aunt, Lily Mausi, and that's my dad." I wait for Quaid to register the people I have mentioned. Manil gets up and Quaid moves to extend his hand to him, but I clutch his elbow and force it down.

Manil starts to walk around the coffee table rapidly. "Quaid is a friend," I say reassuringly.

I turn my head slightly to look at Quaid. His body is still leaning towards Manil.

Lily Mausi is propelling herself up from the couch. After she stands, the couch bears the pear shaped imprint of her buttocks. It's like she is in the habit of leaving a part of herself behind. She is wearing a floral nightie. When I left the house in the morning she had been wearing the same nightie. Her short gray hair is tousled and curls around her face. Her burnt toast eyes dart frantically around.

There is an awkward silence filled with audible thoughts.

Lily Mausi asks Quaid to sit.

Dad starts to stand up, but is a little unsteady and falls right back on the couch.

Quaid looks unsettled.

"Quaid?" Dad booms out, beckoning him closer. "Is you first name Dennis then?" Dad laughs, but no one finds it funny.

Quaid walks over and stands awkwardly to one side of the couch, careful to avoid stepping into Manil's orbit.

"So what do you do, Quaid?"

"Let him sit down first, Pavan, where are your manners?" admonishes my aunt.

My father glares at her.

"I'm a doctor, Sir," Quaid responds.

Manil is still circling the table, careful to avoid eye contact. His body seems to have retracted and he appears smaller than he was, as though he is shrinking into the distance.

It is a relief to me that my secret is now out in the open.

"Quaid, Muslim?" Dad asks.

"Yes, sir, I am Muslim," he says and I've encountered that defensiveness before.

"No need to take that tone," my father says. "Once my closest friend was Abdul Haider, a Muslim fellow. He was nicknamed Hyde, that's what we called him. This was back in my Calcutta Law School days. Hyde and I would memorize the Constitution by swimming laps across the College Square pool. Those laws had complicated language." He shakes his head and sighs.

"There are 1.5 billion Muslims in the world and 1 billion Hindus. Saudi Arabia, Somalia and Oman have the highest concentration of Muslims and Indonesia, Pakistan and India have the most number of Muslims ..."

"Manil, look at me, say hello to Quaid," I say in a firm voice, interrupting the flow of awkward statistics.

Without slowing down, looking or pausing, Manil asks, "Hello Quaid, are you from Pakistan or India?"

Everyone says Manil and I have the same eyes and the same smile. The difference I know is his exhaustive honesty. I wonder if Quaid has fathomed our depths as yet.

"Sit down, Quaid," Lily Mausi exhorts once again. "Are you hungry? I have some éclairs from the patisserie down the street."

He complies sitting where Lily Mausi had sat. His body descends into the hollow of her previous presence.

"So Quaid how do you know Mira?" Dad asks.

"Quaid works at the Holy Hope, Dad," I interject before Quaid can respond. "He's in urgent care. He helped me when I fell and twisted my ankle and then we became friends. And one thing led to another and here we are today."

"When did you twist your ankle, Mira?" Lily Mausi asks from the kitchen.

"Oh, about a year ago, Mausi."

"Lily twisted her ankle 10 months and 27 days ago. I remember because she did not come to pick me up from school that day and Mrs. Ruben asked me to get into her car, but I refused and Mrs. Ruben got angry and complained to Mira and Mira sent a taxi to pick me up. The license plate of the taxi was 6UQY132. The taxi was yellow and I don't like things that are yellow, so I refused to get in the taxi and Mrs. Ruben called Mira again who called her friend Marjorie Smith to pick me up. Marjorie has a blue car and I like the color blue and Marjorie has blue eyes and I like the color of Marjorie's eyes and Marjorie has brown hair. Are you from India?"

"Where are you from, Quaid?" Dad asks.

"I grew up in Seattle, Sir. My parents are from Kuwait, Manil."

Lily Mausi has come out of the kitchen carrying a plate of éclairs. She stops near the dining table and looks frozen in place with the plate in her hand. Quaid goes up, takes the plate from her and sets it down on the table.

Manil has increased his pace and is virtually running around the coffee table. There is no stopping him. Sheer exhaustion will finally slow him down, but for now I have to allow him this release.

I am aware that everything Quaid is witnessing is coming as a surprise to him. I had told him very little about my family. All I had mentioned was that ours was a nest of insecurities.

That summer, a year ago, when I first met him, I was running from the third floor to the children's ward on the second floor of the Holy Hope Hospital when I slipped and fell down the stairs. I lay at the bottom of the stairs, my ankle twisted under me. He was passing by and having witnessed my fall stopped to examine my swelling ankle, and prescribed "a leg up." His fingers had been gentle and his eyes gentler. I'd never seen him before. He would have registered if I had. I loved his humility and the red flag of his religion. He held that before him wherever he went. I watched him introduce himself to a patient once. He introduced his name, his discipline and his religion all in one breath.

His fingers were long and bony; his hair cropped military style; his eyes were dark and deep set and his mouth wide and generously shaped. He was a little taller than me and through his scrubs I could make out a metro thin tie. When he smiled at me that day, his teeth glistened white and meticulous. He struck me with his professional gallantry.

I was conscious of my own appearance, long straight hair, wrapped carelessly into a thick braid. Wisps of hair had escaped confinement and were floating untidily. I was, and am, too short, too thin, too dark, and too intense.

"Hello," he said that day, "I'm Quaid." No other tags.

I held on to his shoulder and breathed out through the throbbing pain, "I'm Mira and hurting."

I sat down on the couch while he attended to me. I

looked down at his bent head and realized that anything could happen. I thought I was inured to the silliness of romance. As a nurse I had registered many failed ones. Empty patient bedsides, nurses crying into their soy lattes and teenage trauma victims glaring defiantly at their parents. But in the intensity of my own reaction I found the thread of insatiability. I already craved his heat.

From that point on it was easy to bump into him fortuitously. He is gorgeous, conceded my friend Marjorie, but what do you know of him?

His family, he explained, had been living in Sammamish for over 20 years. His father was employed for the last fifteen years as an engineer at Cray. His mother was a math teacher at the Sammamish High School, the school where he and his sister had attended. His sister, Reza, had studied marketing at Reed College and was working at Babeland, a sex toys boutique. I had laughed when Quaid told me where Reza worked and Quaid had looked blankly at me.

“Is he your boyfriend then?” Lily Mausi whispers on her way back to the kitchen. Lily Mausi is fond of labels. In her own life she has never managed to acquire the defining one of mother.

“Sort of,” I answer

“Is he religious?” she asks.

"I believe he is a believer."

She shakes her head. "But he grew up in Seattle," she says.

It is as though Dad has heard Lily Mausi, for he asks, "Seattle, huh? Good coffee."

Manil starts to give statistics about Seattle coffee.

I chance a glance at Quaid, afraid to see a reaction, any reaction. Here in these rooms was where my vulnerabilities reposed.

Quaid is looking at Manil. He turns his head and catches my glance.

We meet everyday after work. Mausi gives me a lecture on the virtues of virginity. Her mouth twists into a moue of disgust when she cautions me against the dirtiness of sex and the horrors of exposure. Especially with someone like him, she tacks at the end of her warning. I remain heedless of her caution.

I ask Quaid if Lily Mausi is like his mother. "No, my mother is a teacher," he responds. I agonize over whether Lily Mausi is different because she doesn't work or doesn't work as a teacher. It seems as though Quaid has pegged Lily Mausi's adding and deducting skills.

We often lie in the bed in his apartment. The place

is covered with books and magazines, garments are strewn across the floor in his bedroom and the bed is frequently unmade. It is unlike my room, which is always neat with the eiderdown folded precisely. Only one corner of his bedroom remains clean and clear. This is by his prayer rug.

I find myself straightening his apartment every time I go over. Quaid sits on the couch watching me. Only when the bed is made again do I lie down on it.

"What do your parents say about me?" I ask.

His eyes close in ecstasy and he groans loudly before collapsing over me. "Why do you ask me these questions at these moments? I told them you were a gorgeous woman with mocha skin and chocolate eyes."

"Don't," I implore.

Lying back on the pillows, his chest gleaming with sweat, he responds quietly, deliberately. "Their opinion of you without having met you hinges on your culture. But, once they know you as a person, religion and culture will become mere extractions of your history."

The morning sunlight brightens the dullness of his textured ceiling and I marvel at how our bodies fit so perfectly together, synchronous in movement and in stillness.

Once, a few years ago, Mausi had sat me down and told me how to deal with Dad. She had assured me that everything would be ok, as long as the TV was on. He's had to lead a tough life, she had said in excuse. Dad had been unable to find work as a lawyer after moving to the United States and had instead found a job as a pesticide sprayer. Then a dog in one of his clients' home had died due to pesticide inhalation and the family had sued the company Dad worked for. Dad had been fired and since then had found few jobs that fit his idea of what a back-home lawyer should be doing.

The real truth is that Mausi loves to watch television all day. She once claimed to have learned English through television. She told me that she practiced saying the words with her lower lip stretched over her teeth to make sure she had the right twang. She could swear a blue streak when needed, especially when Chivas Regal appeared after the sun set every evening. But it was our ritual, her swearing, him drinking, and Manil rocking gently.

Lily Mausi is good with Manil. She walks with him to the drugstore down the street so that the neighborhood boys don't make fun of him. She helps him cross the street and tie his laces. She helps him bake cookies in the middle of the night and teaches him how to ignore loud street noises.

Dad isn't a bad man. In fact everyone in the family blames his drinking on the circumstances in his life, my mother dying in childbirth and my brother being the way he is. Yet I have recollections of Dad drinking before Manil was born. Friends would always rationalize his behavior. Too often I heard, "he was once so handsome!" or "he was always well-dressed," or "he was so smart," as though the fact that he was all those things in the past somehow excused his present.

Dad had stopped looking for a job after I got mine. My salary didn't cover much, but it paid for our curry and cabbage living.

Lily Mausi sees me come home bleary-eyed one morning and knows that it is not a late night shift that has kept me out. "Were you doing it with that Muslim prison boy then?" she demands.

"Leave me alone, Mausi, I'm tired," I tell her wearily.

"Decent girls come back home at night," Dad yells at me the same day, before the flush of his pain has receded from his eyes. "Thank God, your mother is dead. What kind of job is this that you do, cleaning the shit and piss off sick people."

On television the documentary narrator is speaking in a flat tone of voice that seems like the sound of my heartbeat monitor.

I surf the Babeland website and call the Seattle number. A woman picks up the phone and I place my order.

"Last night Manil had one of his episodes and tore a clump of his hair out." Lily Mausi says a few days later.

"Why?" I ask.

"On the *National Geographic* channel, they aired a clip of India's mendicant population. I didn't pay attention and couldn't stop it in time."

I go to my brother who is sitting on the floor against the bedroom wall, the bedroom we both share. I put my back against the wall and slither into place beside him. Usually that would make him laugh. We sit together for an hour without saying a word while I absorb him into myself. Then at the end he turns around with his brilliant full-mouthed smile and exclaims at how much he missed me. His love has always hurt me immensely. Today, it seems infinitely worse.

A few days later, Dad has a problem with urination. His stomach becomes bloated and I take him in to the hospital. He is diagnosed with cirrhosis of the liver. While at the hospital he suffers a stroke.

When he is out of critical care, Dad complains

incessantly about wanting his old friend, Mr. Regal. Hospital rules, I explain, pretending indignation. An old friend of my dad stops by the hospital one evening. He shakes his head as he examines my dad's lean frame. "He used to be so handsome," he says, shaking his head.

He was a good dad, all said and done. When I was younger, he'd pull me on to his lap and call me his Mini Mee. I would nuzzle his neck smelling Old Spice and yesterday's drink. Then we'd solve the day's word jumbles together. Four jumbled up words that we had to realign and make sense of.

Quaid invites me to dinner with his sister and her boyfriend, who are visiting him for the weekend. The boyfriend watches me with a half-grin. His white skin seems like a no-color amidst the browns. Quaid's sister, Reza, looks like a feminine version of Quaid.

"So your brother has Asperger's?" Reza asks without much preamble, lighting a cigarette from her boyfriend's.

"Reza!" Quaid says warningly.

"Don't you remember that boy in our school, Quaid? I watched him hitting his head on his locker repeatedly screaming some gibberish. The school counselor had to come to make him stop. But I'm sure your brother is not that bad."

"Reza," Quaid scolds again and the name sounds like razor.

"What? This is why this world is all screwed up. You express sympathy and you get scolded. You don't mind my asking, do you, Mira?"

"There's no need for sympathy, Reza," I say calmly. "We are grateful for my brother."

"I've heard that people like your brother are socially maladjusted."

Reza's boyfriend giggles.

"Oh, fuck! Who the hell cares!" Reza says, grinding out her cigarette. The boyfriend runs his hand down her thigh.

The spinach lasagna and salad taste like sawdust after that.

As Reza and I are stacking dishes in the sink, she looks, winks and says, "I hope you're enjoying your toy." Then her attention is diverted to her brother's sloppy arrangement of jars on the shelves. I've always found winks difficult to execute and these jabbing, conversational winks have particularly confounded me.

I cannot sleep that night. Manil is snoring on his twin bed. I get up and open my underwear drawer and take out the pink package labeled Babeland. I open it and take out the vibrator. I try to turn it on and realize it needs batteries. I put it back into its package and return it to its hiding spot.

"This morning I saw some gulls settle on our windowsill, the time has come then," Lily informs me in her sing-song, serious voice. She extends her plump arms to me and we embrace.

At the hospital Quaid calls out my name as I'm standing outside my father's hospital room. It seems as though he's going to ask me a question, but he doesn't. It is a moment framed by the sound of frantic running, beeping and crying two rooms down.

He hurries on down the hallway and his retreating back looks like a stranger's.

That afternoon it is clear that Dad's looking worse. He continues to complain that if he could only get a drink everything would be much better. Lily Mausi calls him a fucking drunk.

Quaid stops by and sees us gathered together in the hospital room. He walks in and reads Dad's chart hung by the bed, then he stands behind me and rests his hand on my shoulder. I tense up and his hand drops.

"Muslims walk differently," Lily Mausi says, observing Quaid as he walks out of Dad's room.

At home, Manil's movements are frantic. He pulls out the Chivas Regal bottle from the cupboard in the reading area and places it in front of Dad's place on the sofa and rocks back and forth. After he goes to bed, Lily Mausi empties the bottle in the sink.

Back at the hospital that night, Dad's breathing crackles noisily. Quaid sits with me for a while. I ask him why Reza seems to dislike me. Quaid's forehead furrows deeply while he searches for an answer. "Mira, that's not important," he answers finally. "You have other things to worry about at the moment."

I'm not entirely sure Quaid is referring to my father's condition.

He shakes his head. "It's like peeling an onion with you, Mira. Layers upon layers. Nothing is as it seems."

When Dad finally breathes his last, it is 2 a.m and I'm alone in the room. Even after he is gone, I don't alert anyone. I sit in the dark. When the footsteps arrive at the door, my features have aligned themselves again.

On my way back home, I feel like I'm driving through a thickening night with the wind pulling at the car. I am fiercely controlling the steering wheel, determined to stay on track.

I stop by the all-night drugstore, turn off the engine, and sit in my car planning how I will break the news to

Manil. A watery trickle dampens my cheeks and I taste salt. There's a raw feeling in my throat. I take my phone out and text Quaid: heart of onion - peel, cut, dice or slice. Am yours.

I walk into the store and pick up a bottle of Chivas Regal. At the counter, the sales clerk asks me, "There's a sale on batteries this week. Ending tomorrow. Do you want to pick some up?"

Indian Summer

(A Play in One Act)

Characters:

AMOOMA – grandmother,

SHINY – daughter,

MA – also called ELI

DAD – also called CHANDY

Scene: *In the kitchen of a single family, four-bedroom ranch style home in Sunnyvale. The house is in a cul-de-sac adjoining a park. The house smells of fried onions and island breeze potpourri. A round dining table has a bursting backpack, a chemistry book lying open, and a glass of milk on it. There are two chairs at the table. One other chair is at the corner of the room. The fourth chair is near the patio door. A pile of books and a newspaper is stacked up on a small triangular corner table by the chair. There is a small reading lamp shedding the impression of light. In the kitchen, the stovetop is littered with the spluttering fragments of lunch. There is a rag cloth by the stove, which looks used and dirty. It is displayed on the counter as the happy proof of cleanliness. An overhead chandelier is always lit. There are greasy imprints of hands and fingers on the wall near the patio. The floor is white vinyl with blue veins and the kitchen counter is white corian with three burn stains. There are three wooden coasters placed on the burnt spots.*

It is about 5:30p.m. on a Tuesday afternoon. The patio door has been pushed all the way open and it looks as though it is off its rails. There is the feeling of a breeze but no visible sign of it.

At the rise of the curtain Shiny is seated at the table, her Chemistry book is open and she is writing in her notebook, periodically checking her textbook as she writes. Amooma sits on the chair near the patio door. Dad has just walked in and he finds his place on the chair in the corner. He begins to read the newspaper by the light of the lamp near the chair, squinting at the words often. Ma is at the stove making a grilled cheese sandwich. It is a too warm day and the heat of the stove brings sweat beads to Ma's forehead. She is a 5'2" woman, a little rounded around her middle with a gently broad rear end. Her face, which once had been all angles, is now all curves. Lines of anxiety have become etched on her forehead. Nevertheless she hardly looks her age. She has an alertness, a quality control aspect about her. Her eyes dart about registering every movement in the room.

Shiny is a pretty girl, about 16 years old, tall and rangy with arms that hang all the way to her knees. She has a dark complexion that her American friends envy and her Indian friends pity. Her hair, held away from her face with a thick brown hair band, bursts out behind her head. Her cell phone buzzes every few minutes. Each buzz makes Ma's lips tighten.

Dad/Chandy is tall and slender and dressed in a pair of brown slacks and checked white and green half sleeved shirt. He has a thick swathe of graying black hair that he sweeps away from his forehead. There is an air of meticulous neatness about him. His eyes have the habitual glaze of distraction.

Amooma sits at her appointed spot. Her English is heavily accented, a hasty garland of key words. She has lately decided to speak only in English since her grandkids do not know Malayalam. She is wearing a sari with a crumpled, grimy, moth eaten black shawl flung around her shoulders. It is a shawl that has the smell of old. Her face is round and her cataract operated eyes gaze out like half burnt coals, gray and ashy. Her wrinkled, pudgy hands tremble slightly as she adjusts her shawl continuously. It is an Indian Summer day.

Amooma (*in a placatory tone*): "Drrink your milk, Shiny."

Shiny (*without looking up from what she's doing*): "Ma, can you tell Amooma that I'm not five years old."

Amooma (*working the ends of the shawl with her fingers*): "I read. You think I not? Books and TV talk important milk for teenager."

Ma: "Did you have any tests today, Shiny?"

Shiny: "Hmm"

Ma: "Is that a yes or a no?"

Shiny: "Why do *you* need to know? You always need to know *everything*."

Ma: "Why do *I* need to know? Do you hear that Chandy? Your daughter asks why I need to know. Can you answer her? Who pays her bills? She brings a report card studded with Bs and she asks why I need to know! Are you listening, Chandy?"

Dad (*consolingly*): "Shiny, listen to your mother."

Amooma (*nodding her head up and down*): "If drrink milk, mind imprrove, get A grrade."

Ma: "Did you hear your father, Shiny?"

Shiny (*with a grin*): "He just wants you off his back like I do."

Amooma: "and no prroblems with back later."

Dad (*gruffly*): "Shiny."

Ma: "I know what this is. You didn't do well in your test. Isn't that right? Did you study over the weekend? Which subject?"

Shiny: "Interfere, interfere, interfere. This is my life. You don't seem to understand that. And for the record, it wasn't as though you were brilliant in high school!"

Ma (*a bit shocked*): "At least I tried."

Shiny (*sniggering*): "Yes, tried to land a boyfriend."

Amooma (*turns to look at Ma with somber emphasis*): "Eli wild girrrl."

Ma (*exasperated*): "I wasn't wild, Amma. I didn't conform to your conservative ideas."

Shiny (*grinning*): "Do you ever listen to yourself?"

Ma (*turns off the stove and places the sandwich on a plate, looking irritated*): "My situation is not the same as yours. My parents wanted me to get married by the time I finished college."

Shiny (*caustically*): "So you got married when you finished college, didn't you?"

Ma: "After I'd worked for a few years."

Shiny: "Did that really make a difference? Look at you!

Amooma (*with her mouth pursed*): "Boys afterrr Eli because she look like milk, fairr and lovely."

Ma (*in a hurt tone*): "Let's see you make the life that I made."

Shiny (*puts her pen down and closes her book. She flexes her fingers and in a determined voice*): "If you haven't realized it yet, let me tell you that my life will be better than yours. It's either about your weight or your children! I'm not going to end up like you!

Ma (*not knowing how to respond, resorts to addressing Chandy. There is a lump in her throat as she says*): "Read your *New York Times*, Chandy! What difference does it make that your daughter is out of control. What's the latest news item that is absorbing you? Underwear bombs?"

Dad (*lowers the newspaper and obediently*): "Shiny, there's no call to be disrespectful."

Shiny: "Dad, in this country respect is to be earned. (*in a more conciliatory tone*) Besides, Ma knows how to annoy."

Dad (*lifts the newspaper up to his face, blocking the rest of the people in the room from view*): "You two deal with this and leave me out of it, please."

Amooma (*looking at her wrists*): "My doctorr she say milk good for bones."

Ma (*huffily*): "So, I'm fat and lazy? Is that what you just said? I'd like to see *you* have kids and maintain your figure."

Shiny (*pulls the plate close to her and takes a bite of the sandwich*): "*I'll* get back to working out as soon as I give birth."

Ma (*using the rag cloth*): "Yes, sure. Between taking care of two kids and sleeplessness."

Shiny (*argumentatively*): "Others have done more *and* maintained themselves."

Ma (*in a louder voice*): "They've had tummy tucks."

Shiny (looking at her mother's figure dismissively): "So why the hell haven't you got one?"

Ma: "It's too much money and don't you think it suggests vanity and self-obsession? (*switching to her parenting voice*) And stop swearing."

Shiny (*gently*): "Hell is not a bad word, Ma, and Dad, tell Ma to get a tummy tuck."

Dad (*placatingly*): "Shiny, these are not things we talk about openly."

Amooma (*shaking her head and glaring at Ma*): "Your mother no drrink milk in Shiny prregnant. She say milk make her throw up, vimit. That's why *you* not like it, Shiny. I told her. She no listen. If Eli drrink milk, that glass be empty, instead brring flies."

Shiny (*looking at her newspaper shielded Dad*): "Why don't we talk about it openly?"

Ma: "Tummy tucks mess with nature."

Shiny (*exasperatedly*): "Dad!"

Dad: "What? I already told you that we don't talk about tummy tucks openly. That's between your mother and her surgeon."

Ma (*in a horrified gasp*): "What does that mean? You want me to get a tummy tuck? Is that what you're saying, Chandy?"

Shiny (*sarcastically smiling*): "Listen to Dad!"

Dad: "Now, Eli. Don't impute motives here."

Ma (*with a short wild laugh as she throws the soiled cloth into the trash violently*): "I know what this is!

Your Dad thinks I'm fat, you think I'm frumpy and my mother thinks I'm wild."

Shiny (*smiling*): "I'd rather go with wild."

Ma (*shaking her head at her daughter*): "That's where you're headed Shiny. It's not something to joke about. "

Amooma: "Milk do a complexion good. Comparre Eli yours complexion, Shiny."

Shiny (*whiningly*): "Ma, can you tell her to stop. My complexion is not dark because of lack of milk."

Ma (*with a sly smile)*: "Are you sure? Look at all the foods we Indians eat. Everything is colored yellow and brown. Look at the food these Americans eat, white cheese, white pasta, white bread, white eggs, white fish, white chicken, white clam chowder..."

Amooma: "...and white milk"

Shiny (*frustratedly*): "That is complete nonsense. What about red meat, does that make people red?"

Ma: "Red meat eaters look red and flushed. It's a question of how much. If your entire diet consisted of red meat, you would become red."

Shiny: "What about genetics?"

Ma *(smiling)*: "If I had to carry that argument further, genetics determines what gets put on your plate. You would be fairer if we had American food all the time. But our palate is given to Indian flavors."

Shiny (*viciously*): "I hate Indian food."

Ma (*in a softer, more mellow tone*): "Once you go to college, you'll realize how much you love it. I've heard that kids in college come back to their eating roots."

Shiny (*scoffingly*): "So I'm dark because you force me to eat Indian food?"

Dad (*folding the newspaper in half lengthwise*): "What is this? You are beautiful just the way you are, child."

Shiny and Ma together (*in an annoyed tone*): "Dad!" "Chandy"

Ma: "But, really! What's wrong with your complexion, Shiny?"

Amooma: "In my countrry, rrich people wash hairr in milk. You put milk on face in earrly morrning and become brighter. And drrink milk cleans inside outside."

Dad (*sitting up and looking at Amooma, who ignores him*): "Dark is beautiful. What is this obsession with fairness? Leave her alone!"

Shiny (*accusingly*): "You married fair, Dad."

Ma (*laughing sarcastically*): "I'm fair, fat, frumpy and wild."

Dad (*sinking back into his chair wearily*): "You really need to stop putting yourself down. It's a little tiresome."

Shiny (*nodding her head*): "If you'd gotten a tummy tuck, you wouldn't be so down on yourself."

Ma: "Oh! Are we back to the tummy tuck again?"

Shiny: "Just saying."

Ma: "A bit too much. When did this become about me? In this family only he has ever supported me."

(*Shiny and Dad share a glance*)

Amooma (shaking her head from side to side, the shimmer of water in her eyes): "Miss my poorr Georgius. He love milk, good to his Amooma, poorr Georrgius."

Ma: "I don't want to talk about him. It was a mistake to bring him up."

Shiny (*too loudly*): "Stop it!"

Dad (*surprised*): "What is going on?"

Ma: "Whenever Georgie is mentioned, you fly off the handle."

Shiny (*glaring*): "You use his name as a weapon against me."

Ma (*throwing her hands up*): "Was it Amooma or me? Either way, there's no need to yell. Anyway, what did I just say? I have a special bond with Georgie, like mothers and sons do. For one, he didn't argue with me as much."

Shiny (*with a hurt grin*): "He is your perfect child, isn't he?"

Ma (*frowning*): "Were you jealous of him, Shiny?"

Dad (*looking stressed*): "I don't like where this is going. Let it go. Constant bickering ... can a man not enjoy a quiet evening reading the newspaper?"

Amooma: "Georgius is a fair boy. Why, I ask?"

Shiny (*with tears in her eyes*): "Right from the time, we were babies, you always took his side against me. If we were fighting over a toy, he always got it. If we were arguing, I was the one to get punished. In school, no matter what grade he brought home, it was always ok, whereas I could always do better..."

Ma (*dismissively*): "That's ridiculous. I was always surprised by how belligerent you were towards your brother."

Shiny (*shouting*): "You made me like that, Ma! If only

you'd been a bit fairer."

Amooma: "Eli fairer than anyone in her school!"

Ma: "So are you happy now?"

Shiny (*in a deep guttural voice*): "Happy as in gay, Ma?"

Ma (*shaking her head*): "Sophomoric puns."

Shiny: "Well he's the one who's gay. I wish *I* was lesbian."

Ma (*looking up towards the ceiling*) "What did I do to deserve this? You live your life giving your kids the best years of your life and all you get back in return are accusations. I wish I had left you two to the babysitter and taken up a job. Maybe you'd be normal then."

Shiny (*with sudden savagery)*: "If you haven't realized it as yet, I'm the one who's (*using her fingers to mime the quotes*) normal."

Ma (*as though Shiny hadn't spoken*): "When he came back from college, I could smell it in him, you know."

Shiny: "How do gay people smell, Ma?"

Amooma: "Apupa always say, an apple a day keep healthy and wise. I say wun glass of milk a day keep happy and gay."

Shiny (*sarcastically*): "It is truth day."

Ma: "There is no greater truth than unhappiness."

Dad (*with a pinched look around his mouth*): "What nonsense is all this, Eli?"

Shiny: "Why? Because our beloved Georgie Georgius is gay? He's not dead and gone, you know."

Ma: "You won't understand, Shiny."

Shiny (*venomously*): You, with your ridiculous ego. Get over it. Georgie's gay, very gay. For the record, I've always known that about him. You think he's done you some great big hurt. Well, it's not about you. It's not about us. It's not about Amooma's milk and it's not about unhappiness."

Dad (his voice rising): "Stop it, both of you!"

Amooma: Shiny drrink milk, calm you.

Ma (*bursting out*): "leave her be, leave her be, leave her be. Can't you stop your non-stop haranguing? It's driving me nuts! (*then looking at Shiny*) So you don't think I have anything to be sorry about?"

Amooma's face crumples and she slowly gets up. The creases of her skin line up one on top of the other. It's a terrible thing to watch, her distress. She slowly, heavily leaves the room.

Shiny (*looks at her mother angrily*): "What's wrong with you?"

Ma: "I didn't mean to yell at her, she drove me to it! It's all this talk about Georgie. You don't seem to have any boundaries. He's finding himself in college. So be it. I'm patient."

Shiny: "Is that how you're going to deal with it? By the way, let me break it to you that he's not going to 'change.' So much for your patience! And one day when your friend, Leona Aunty, asks you why he hasn't married as yet, what are you going to tell her?"

Ma: "It's none of Leona's business and neither is it yours how I deal with my son."

Shiny: "He's my brother! And I say let's celebrate his gayness with a come-out party! Never been done before, has it? Especially not in your Indian community."

Ma: "You must ridicule everything and grease every word with sarcasm. I won't have it!"

Shiny (*smiling sweetly while texting*): "Mommy dearest."

Ma: "And STOP TEXTING!"

Shiny: "Guess who I'm texting, Ma? Your gorgeous Georgious. What were you thinking of anyway to give him a name like that? Queer!"

Dad (*throwing the rolled up newspaper violently at the wall, but it falls short, fluttering apart*): "I've had it! I've had it! I cannot live in this house anymore! I cannot bear it!"

He stands up. His eyes look wild and he opens and closes his mouth as he stands there glaring at Ma and Shiny. Ma looks down. Shiny starts to cry.